Lord Carlisle's Enticing Lure

Scarlett Affairs
Book 5

Cerise DeLand

DRAGONBLADE PUBLISHING, INC.

ARE YOU SIGNED UP FOR DRAGONBLADE'S BLOG?

You'll get the latest news and information on exclusive giveaways, exclusive excerpts, coming releases, sales, free books, cover reveals and more.

Check out our complete list of authors, too!

No spam, no junk. That's a promise!

Sign Up Here

www.dragonbladepublishing.com

Dearest Reader;

Thank you for your support of a small press. At Dragonblade Publishing, we strive to bring you the highest quality Historical Romance from some of the best authors in the business. Without your support, there is no 'us', so we sincerely hope you adore these stories and find some new favorite authors along the way.

Happy Reading!

CEO, Dragonblade Publishing

Additional Dragonblade books by Author Cerise Deland

Scarlett Affairs Series
Lord Ashley's Beautiful Alibi (Book 1)
Lord Ramsey's Red-Headed Ruin (Book 2)
Lord Appleby's Gorgeous Imposter (Book 3)
Lord Fournier's Shameless Princess (Book 4)
Lord Carlisle's Enticing Lure (Book 5)

Matrimony! Series
If I Loved You (Book 1)
Because of You (Book 2)
You Made Me Love You (Book 3)

Naughty Ladies Series
Lady, Be Wanton (Book 1)
Lady, Behave (Book 2)
Lady, No More (Book 3)
Lady, You're Mine (Book 4, Novella)

The Lyon's Den Series
The Lyon's Share
The Lyon's Perfect Mate
Lie Down With a Lyon

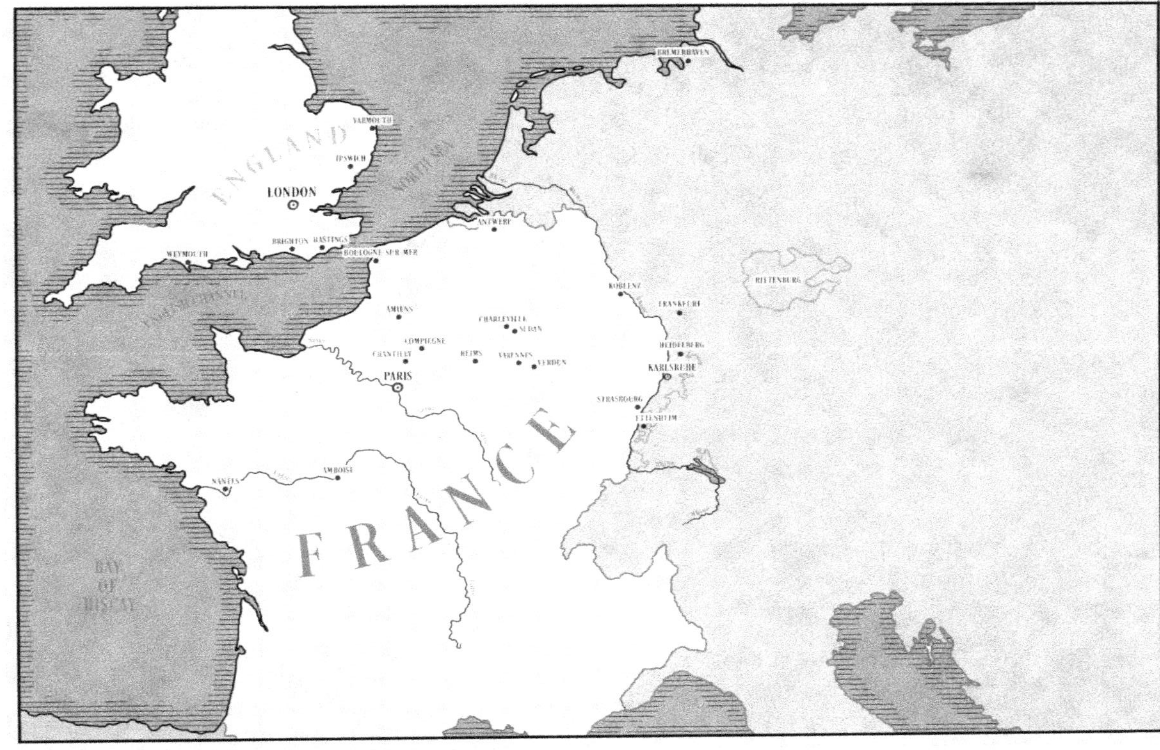

FRANCE
ENGLAND
NORTH SEA
ENGLISH CHANNEL
BAY OF BISCAY
LONDON
PARIS
YARMOUTH
IPSWICH
BRIGHTON
HASTINGS
WEYMOUTH
BOULOGNE SUR MER
ANTWERP
BREMERHAVEN
KOBLENZ
FRANKFURT
HEIDELBERG
KARLSRUHE
STRASBOURG
ETTENHEIM
AMIENS
CHARLEVILLE
SEDAN
COMPIEGNE
CHANTILLY
REIMS
VARENNES
VERDUN
NANTES
AMBOISE
RIETENBURG

Chapter One

June 16, 1805
Brighton, England

CLIVE DAVENPORT COULDN'T believe his eyes.

He took a few steps closer to the vision in pink and lavender. She stood silhouetted against the sweet blue sky, motionless, facing the sea, her head thrown back, her midnight hair billowing around her as the wind off the Channel buffeted her whole, slender body. But she did not move. Arms out, she fought the force, then let it sway her. She seemed so determined and yet so ethereal that she did not even seem to breathe.

"Papa! Papa!" His daughter of three gazed at the lady, too.

He was certain, however, what attracted Annabelle was the lady's kite.

"Birdie!" the child exclaimed, tugging on his hand. She flapped one arm as if she would fly away.

"Well, my poppet, I'd introduce us, but we do not know the lady." *Only I know of her. And only by her actions.* When had she come to Brighton? And where were her sketchpads and pencils? She always had some to hand. "We're going for cake and ices, remember?"

His little girl pouted. "I want t' fly."

He winced. He hated to go, now that he had sight of this lady and an opportunity to make her acquaintance. He'd been

1

intrigued by this beauty when first he saw her. Spotting her near his Richmond country house on the Thames, he'd been drawn by her elfin form. Black hair, large, gamin eyes, dainty limbs—she'd appeared on the banks of the river most mornings in fair weather and in not so fair. Arriving early, before nine usually, she'd set up her chair, easel, a few large palettes, and basket of paints about her on the grassy knoll above the flow of the river. Before she began her sketching, she'd walk to the river's edge and, bending, trail her fingers in the ripples of the water. February was no time to be outside for long. The forest along the Thames could be thick and sheltering, but the wind could cut through one's coat and make one yearn for a cozy fire and hot tea.

Yet this lady, petite as she was, had fortitude. Braving the cold, she had remained to sit and paint for at least one hour, more often two. She would snuggle in a sturdy coat, a forest-green redingote that draped about her legs as if she were receiving subjects. The coat blended so well into the evergreens that even with his superb binoculars, Clive, at first attempt to spot her, often mistook her for part of the woods. Still, he'd had to hunt for her each morning. He'd walk along the Thames. Find her newest spot. Then debate with himself if he should introduce himself.

But then one morning as February turned to March when she had come closer to his house, sighting her through his magnified lenses, he saw she painted a verdant forest. Watercolors of pale limes and verdant greens, browns and umbers, adorned her canvas. Her forest along a silvery, flowing river was a dark, deep mystery. Even from afar, he was called to it. Yet propriety had pulled him back, resisting the pull of her artistry.

Then as days passed, he noted something odd. Two things, really. The first was that she switched from painting her forest scenes to using charcoal to draw towns. Buildings. Nothing he could identify. It was as if she practiced a town upon a coastline, sketching quickly a house, a cottage, a shop nearby, then a Palladian mansion.

The second thing that surprised him was that as the days

warmed, she came to the river only every other day. In late March, she disappeared. He had mourned her loss and his failure to introduce himself.

Certainly, it would have been a pleasure to meet her. Of course, it would have been the polite thing to introduce himself in Richmond.

Even now. He could use his daughter's attraction to her kite as the excuse.

Yet he had stayed back, arguing with himself that he did not need to engage a stranger. Besides, he had work to do. His daughter to amuse. No time for folly. The lady pursued her hobby of kites, amazingly. No need to disturb her.

Now, in warm and sultry June, he admired her for another rare reason. Her abandon to the bounties of sun and sky and sea stirred a growing elemental need in his own life. One he could not define except to say he needed something new and invigorating to his days. Something to amuse and fulfill his lonely nights.

"Papa!" His daughter tugged at his hand in the direction of the lady. "Fly!"

He should take Bella's interest in the thing and introduce himself. Finally.

Yet the reason he'd stayed away from her, the reason he did not introduce himself, was clear. Simple and frail.

Then and now, her looks should mean nothing. Five years ago, he'd sworn off any attractions to pretty women. Bitter experience had taught him lessons he vowed to follow for the rest of his days. This woman might lure him, but he had no illusions about how a gorgeous pair of eyes could tempt and a pretty set of lips could lie. He preferred humble girls. Plain, with education and a small measure of wit.

That first time he had noticed her and every time thereafter, she had her drawing supplies with her. Every time thereafter, she put pencils, paper, or a tray of a few watercolors to dedicated use. Today, though, she was without. He could question why, but then his head and his heart—like his daughter's—were filled with her amusement of her kite. A small bit of red and yellow, the thing remained aloft.

As if she too marveled at her abilities, she suddenly shook herself to awareness. She turned toward him and Annabelle.

Had she felt his eyes upon her?

No, how could she? I am nothing to her. It's the kite she's concerned about. Or Bella's interest.

His daughter grunted, then stamped her little foot and pulled at his hand.

"Yes, yes. We're going." If he left this shore now, would he find this lady again? He hated to turn toward the town.

But Bella had a different idea. She broke away from him. Wobbling toward the lady over the treacherous little rocks, she stuck out her chubby little arms as if she were a ballerina, and good Lord, was she fast. Certainly, she was quicker than Clive, who was utterly surprised at her!

To his shock, the lady crouched down and threw a huge smile toward Bella. She knew what his baby wanted, and held out the lead to the kite.

Bella raced up and grabbed it. Children this young took what life offered, didn't they?

Her pudgy face up to watch the red paper in the sky, Bella pointed toward the thing that flew like a bird. She giggled as the wind carried her along, her eyes on her only desire.

"Come back!" the lady shouted at her as Bella tried to navigate the rocky beach—and teetered and shook.

He jolted in alarm.

The winds blustered and blew, far stronger than his little girl.

No! Stop! "Bella, come back," he called, but he knew she did not hear him nor have any inclination to obey. He ran toward her, stumbling along the stony shore.

But Bella was enchanted, oblivious to the waves and the danger as she tramped into the water.

A white-capped wave loomed like a monster. Angry, another appeared, five times as tall as his little girl.

"No!" he shouted. His hat flew away. He trudged into the rush, the pull of the undertow battering his legs as he trudged forward to get his girl.

The woman sprang forward, running after Bella, straight into the water.

Bella stumbled, but rose up, smiling and showing it all great fun. She followed the kite and her fascination. She giggled, caring not that she was in the ocean. But then a wave—foamed in white like a wild beast—rose up and rolled over her.

Nooo! Clive tripped. Damn the stones.

A second wave, big as the one that took his girl, rolled toward him. Freezing water filled his boots and soaked his breeches. But he stood, weaving, shaken…struggling to keep his footing.

Determination had him stepping toward the last spot he'd seen his daughter. But…no! He saw no one!

He could not lose her! *Never!*

He dashed deeper into the water, the waves threatening, icy and heavy against him. He saw a sprig of blue and knew it was Bella. A patch of pink and lavender shot up…and stood.

Sodden, reeling, the lady crushed Bella in her arms.

Clive lost his breath. Yet hope swamped him. He struggled to stride nearer to them.

The lady crooned to his daughter, her lips in Bella's wet hair.

He heard her. Nonsense, her words resembled some foreign language, but Clive knew the soothing sounds of love and caring any adult bestowed upon a child, scared and alone.

Bella clung to the lady, her chubby arms clasped tightly around her rescuer's neck.

If she cried, Clive could not tell.

"Thank you, thank you," he managed over and over when he got to them.

Bella left her rescuer's arms and came to his. "Papa." She nuzzled her sweet little face into the hollow of his shoulder.

"I know, sweet one, I know. You're safe." He reached out to the lady, and though she shook, she grabbed his hand. "You are both safe. Let's go in."

Struggling against the lash and pull of the waves, they trudged out of the water up to hot, dry land.

"You're soaked," he said to the lady.

She picked at her muslin gown, but no amount of that would save her from the way the dress clung to her generous breasts and the elegant line of her torso and legs.

His daughter clung to him, soaking the front of his frockcoat. But he had to provide whatever warmth he could for both of them. He put Bella to her feet. "Stand here, my girl." Then he shrugged out of his frockcoat and wrapped it around her. The garment was so huge that the still-dry part of the garment enveloped her. A good thing.

Clive turned to his mystery lady. "Let me give you my waist-coat, miss."

Her teeth chattered and she had trouble saying, *"Non...non, monsieur. It is not necessary."*

"But it is." He already had the thing off and around her. The act covered the fact that he saw her, once more silhouetted against the sunlight, as God had made her. She was wet, perfectly formed, a naked nymph.

She clutched the edges of his waistcoat and closed her eyes, her cheeks coloring in embarrassment even as she shuddered in her sopping-wet clothes.

"Come, allow me to escort you. Where do you live?"

"I have rooms at the Old Ship Hotel. But you should go home, monsieur. Your daughter needs attention."

"Annabelle and I are at the Old Ship, too." Relief swamped his senses. "Let's go up."

"They will wonder at our condition." French, was she? Her accent gave levity to the positive result of their encounter with the elements.

"Indeed!" He laughed at their success and offered his free arm to her to help her navigate the stones and sand. "But I think if we go in together, fewer will decide we are quite mad to have gone for a swim."

She gave a laugh and looped her arm around his. "I agree. Let's hurry."

Chapter Two

GISELLE LAURANT TOOK his arm and strolled beside her rescuer, rejoicing at his quick humor, transfixed by his readiness to save his daughter but also to save *her* life. Up close, he was so devastating. So handsome. His hair was unusual, a light brown with platinum streaks of sunlight. His coloring against the bronze of his skin summoned an appreciation for his undaunted strength and his generosity. Had she seen him before? Where and when could that have been?

She let him lead her up the wooden stairs to the street. Focusing on her relief that the child and she were safe, she smiled that he was so pleased his daughter was unharmed. She knew men who did not bother with the welfare of their daughters…or of their wives, for that matter.

She inhaled, pleased at his graciousness to offer the assurance of his arm, as well as the modesty of his waistcoat. Her newest gown was ruined, but then, she'd have another made. What was a bit of muslin to the value of a child's life? *Or even, yes, my own.*

That caused her to smile more broadly at this man. He had not only rushed to save her life, but made haste to preserve her propriety. So then, a lady's good name was important to him. Another rare but vital quality of any true gentlemen.

And did her other man observe them? She scanned the beach,

her heart quickening for just a few beats. She spied no one else, thank goodness. Her guard did not arise this early in the morning. When she did detect him at his duty, that was usually after noon, when more filled the streets, when he could come upon her easily in a crowd—and stick more closely to her. *If only I did not need him at all...*

She rubbed her arm. The need for this man was accidental—and she appreciated his protection.

Still, being alone, out in the wide world, protected in her work, was a welcome treat she had so rarely tasted. She could feel normal. And at the moment, she had this unique opportunity to appear like any other woman who walked along the street beside a handsome man. Well, yes, she was soaked with seawater, wrapped in his waistcoat, but allowing herself the pleasure of his escort. How often had she enjoyed the opportunity to admire an attractive man and to murmur her thanks for his rescue and his generosity?

"Mademoiselle? You grin but you shiver. Shall we walk faster?" He stepped closer, his smile warm with satisfaction that matched her own.

"Let's try!" She nodded, then hurried beside him, frozen and shivering, her gown clinging to her like a second skin.

But the sun seared her gown and heated her body. Beside his towering from, holding on to his muscular bicep, she could not take her eyes from him. She felt no fear. Thought of no trauma. Nor of her work. Only this rare, marvelous creature. Dapper, broad shouldered, with lean hips, he strode with an easy swagger. His coloring gave him a carefree air. His light-brown hair streaked with the rays of the sun made her think of carousels and games of bowls. His pale eyes that shone brightly from his handsome, tanned face seemed more silver than gray. A vision, tall, sleek, easy on the eyes, he took the world as if he owned it all.

He certainly had captured her imagination. She drew in a huge breath and shook away her fascination. He was no one to her and should remain so. She'd fished his young daughter from the sudden fury of the Channel. He would be grateful. That was normal. Furthermore, she was no one to him—and must remain so. She had work to do, and now would return to it. Dallying with a man like a flirtatious chit would only preoccupy her. She had no time for that.

"Are you here in Brighton on holiday?" He led her up the second flight of wooden steps from the beach to the Grand Parade. In his embrace, his daughter nestled beneath his chin. She was calm, smiling, recovered from the near disaster she seemed to have never comprehended.

"Ah, *oui*. Yes." He would hear her French accent, if he had not already. She did not try to hide it. That took so much effort. She failed at any disguise, having tried it in France, and had had to flee here to survive. "A few weeks. The sea air draws me."

"Annabelle and I as well." They took the steps gingerly. "Tough to climb, eh?" he said as both of them had trouble navigating in sopping-wet clothes.

At the top, they sidestepped carriages and pedestrians, then headed straight across the wide road to the entrance to the hotel. Her time with him ran short. She should rejoice, but once he was gone, she'd feel his lack. He was a man to be treasured. A man one would miss. A man who should be valued. She had known no men like him.

For that reason alone, she had to be free of him.

Inside the reception hall, she stopped to thank him for his kindness to her and began to shrug from his waistcoat. "I'm afraid it is quite ruined."

"No matter." He jostled his little girl in his arms and put up a palm. "You need the warmth. Please. Do wear it to your room."

His warning had her blinking. Then she looked down. She was quite indecent, her body defined by the revealing muslin. "I see. *Merci beaucoup*," she murmured as she wrapped the waistcoat more firmly around her torso.

"We must hurry to ensure none of us catches a chill from this. What room are you in? I can escort you."

"Please, do not bother with me. Your daughter needs you." *Do I sound like a trained parrot?* She turned to the child, sorry to end the little girl's acquaintance so soon. "Goodbye, my dear. Sir? I thank you for everything."

He looked bereft. "Please, allow me to—"

She patted her hip, looking for her little purse, but all she had was that thin, wet muslin clinging to her. Alarmed, she threw up her hands. "Ah, non!"

"What's wrong?"

"I...I just realize I have lost my little reticule in the sea. My coins and my key, they are gone!"

"I'm sure the hotel manager will give you another key. As for your reticule, change quickly and we can both return to search the beach."

"Non, non. Merci beaucoup, monsieur." Oh, now she was so undone she was reverting completely to her native language. Many English hated French. She would hate it if suddenly he were one of them and changed his attitude toward her. "I can find it."

"Sir!" He hailed a man who had just finished with another guest. "This lady has lost her key. Please, a substitute! We had a mishap on the beach and, as you can see, she is freezing and needs to get into her room quickly."

"Your name, my lady?" The receptionist ran his gaze down her disheveled form.

"Madame Laurant, monsieur. Room 122."

Raising a finger, the fellow was spurred to action by the immediacy of need. He scurried behind his formal wall and returned with a large iron key. "Is there anything else I can do for you? A hot bath, perhaps?"

"Oui, later. In an hour, *peut-être?* I must find my little purse and money. Merci beaucoup." Then she turned to her dashing stranger and bade him, "*Au revoir*, monsieur. I remain ever thankful for your help."

Her rescuer stepped with her toward the grand staircase.

"Madame Laurant! *S'il vous plaît.* Do allow me to introduce myself and my daughter."

Oh, that she did not want! She could waste no time with endearing men. "Monsieur…"

"I am Carlisle. Lord Carlisle of Richmond and London and a few other places."

The name…the name sang in her head. Why?

"And this is my daughter, Annabelle Davenport. She likes kites, as well you know. Birds, flowers, too, eh, my chick?" He tickled the girl's tummy, and she curled up in a giggle. "We call her Bella."

"Belle," she corrected her father with a bright-eyed smirk.

Giselle had to give in to such charm. Few had offered it to her in the past decade. She craved it and so she relented. "I am delighted to make your acquaintance, monsieur. And Belle's."

They took the stairs and, of course, he was such a gentleman that he took hold of Giselle's elbow. He was persistent.

Her room was second from the stairs, and in an instant, they stood before her door. She inserted her key and let the door fall open. "Thank you once more, Lord Carlisle. Goodbye, Belle. No more running to the sea without your papa, promise me."

"Promise." The little girl nodded her golden head, her arms still clinging to her father's neck.

Lord Carlisle was not so easily dismissed. He smiled down at Giselle as if he held a marvelous secret that lit his electric-gray eyes. "We are next door."

"How wonderful," she said with less relish than he had announced it. She wished no proximity to lead to any more friendliness.

"Please, will you allow me to invite you and your husband to dinner?"

"Non. I take my meals alone."

"Monsieur Laurant is not with you?"

"Monsieur passed away many years ago, my lord. Many thanks for your generosity. Now, if you don't mind, I must change my clothes."

"Of course." He took a respectful step back. "Please let me know if there is anything I can do for you. Anything at all."

"Thank you. I will." *But you can't.*

Chapter Three

H IS SISTER WAS late.

Clive paced the drawing room floor. Terese was to have arrived from London at four or five o'clock at the latest. Now, at seven forty, she was very late. Most unlike her.

He went to the window once again. His worries about Terese vied with his concern he had about the lady who stayed next door—and whom he could see had stood outside now for more than twenty minutes beneath a hotel brazier lamp.

Madame Laurant was unmistakable in the darkening gloom. What in hell was she doing standing out in that storm? Alone, no less. And at night. She had stood there amid louder and louder thunder. With each shocking crack across the sky, her shoulders hunched.

Rain pattered suddenly against his window. She huddled in her short pelisse as she searched the wide thoroughfare before her. Was she meeting someone? It seemed so.

At once, in a fierce downpour, the rain came. She did not move. Did not seek shelter. Was her need to meet this person so dire that she would risk a complete drenching?

God knew, she'd had enough this morning when she plunged into the sea to save his Bella.

Lightning zagged across the horizon.

Clive had the instinctive urge to run downstairs and throw her over his shoulder. Anything to get her out of the deluge and into shelter.

But he could not do any of that, could he? She was not his to save.

"Not tonight," he told himself, and finished the dram of whisky he'd poured.

In truth, he ought not be so worried about her. She was merely an acquaintance. Her welfare—indeed, her health after her dash into the ocean—should not concern him so deeply. But his mother had suffered from inflammation of the lungs, and he knew the toll a sudden chill could take. Especially on so slight a figure as the exquisite Madame Laurant.

Admit it. Your preoccupation with her is more than for her health or her quick response to save Bella. True, he could not push aside his questions about why she was now in Brighton—and why she'd been in Richmond near his house, so near he could see her from his hilltop study window down to the shore of the flowing Thames. She was the artist whom he had seen so many times through his binoculars. No other woman moved with such grace and alacrity. She certainly resembled that woman, her wealth of ink-black hair, her delicate bone structure as she stood viewing the sea. She had to be the same woman, the same artist, who had told villagers that she had to leave Richmond for Dover and Hastings.

Why did she travel so much? Was she eluding someone, something?

He laughed at that absurdity. She was no criminal, escaping the long arm of a Bow Street officer.

He shifted, his nerves clamoring at that disastrous possibility. *No.* She did not have the look of someone who stole, or worse. Yet she was wary. Of what or whom? He saw her skepticism when she had looked around them on the beach. Had she expected someone to be there? *No.* No, she had relaxed after she looked around and found no one.

He'd love to ask her whom she expected, whom she did not care for. But he could not ask her any of that. He would have to know her better to be so intrusive—and he had little chance of that. When he had probed, even slightly, she had been short with him. So there was that.

He took a drink. He was foolish to focus on her.

Terese was his finer concern—and truth was, she was never late. It was a family trait: She prided herself on her promptness and had trained her staff to follow her lead. But travel from London could present problems. Lame horses, lost carriage wheels, or unskilled grooms could all make any journey a misery. Terese's town carriage and her London-stabled horses were always in tip-top order. Her stable hands were expert, too.

But there was little he could do about her arrival. He'd hope and pray she'd met no calamities. If he heard nothing by noon tomorrow, he would hire a Bow Street Runner and send him out to find her. She usually stopped in Crawley when she came to Brighton, so Clive had that to go on. For now, he would just have to wait for Terese to breeze in, as she always did, like a hurricane.

His gaze drifted across the room to his daughter. Rather than wait any longer for Terese, he'd ring for supper to be sent up for him. He'd have a treat of cake sent up for Bella, who had eaten her supper earlier. He hated eating like a monk in his room, but what could he do? Children did not sup with adults, anywhere, ever, except at home. But he was hungry and she needed to have her dessert and retire—and soon. Bella was happy at the moment. Sitting in the wing chair drawing with her stubby pencil, she pressed her little lips together in concentration. She was a blonde beauty. *Like her mother.*

He spun away from that memory.

Where was the bellpull? Hands on his hips, he gazed around the cozy salon. Usually, a hotel put its pulls in the main rooms. Near windows and draperies. Often near large pieces of furniture like the two credenzas on the far wall. But he'd be darned if he could find it.

Perhaps his bedroom? He strode in and poked around. *No. Bella's?*

Not there either.

What to do?

He winced, hating to disturb Bella to take her downstairs.

"Listen to me, sweetheart." He went to one knee, and her gray eyes met his. "I have to go downstairs to order our supper. I'll be only a minute. Will you just stay here and draw for me?"

She bobbed her head absently, her mind fully on her art.

"Shall I order cake or pudding for dessert?"

Her round face beamed her delight. "Cake and pud."

Laughing, he got to his feet. "Both it is!"

He found his frockcoat, shrugged into it, and shot his cuffs. Then he pocketed the room key, bade her adieu with a promise of, "Only a few minutes." Then he emerged into the empty hall and locked his daughter in. He jogged down the stairs and faced the receptionist, grinning. "I'd like to order supper sent up to my rooms. Have you a menu for the evening?"

"Yes, milord. One minute while we get it from the dining room." He waved a hand to summon one of his footmen, and off that man went to fetch it.

The rain pounded like a thousand needles against the windowpanes.

Clive drummed his fingers on the polished marble desktop. Was madame still outside waiting in the rain? "Terrible storm out there."

"It is, sir. Blew up sudden, like."

Clive tried for nonchalance. "I noticed that Madame Laurant went out recently." *Whom did she meet?*

"Yes, sir, she did."

"Was someone to call for her? With a carriage, perhaps?"

The fellow sent him a weak smile, his attention reluctantly drawn from his paperwork. "I hope so, sir."

So do I. "She didn't want to wait inside for her caller?"

"I guess not, sir. No." The reception clerk disappeared behind a wall of mail slots.

So much for gossipy hotel staff.

The footman appeared with the menu card, and Clive scanned the list of items. He told the footman to send up a main of roast beef and potatoes, with vanilla cake and chocolate pudding for dessert. Just as he would have handed the menu back across the desk, Madame Laurant scurried in the front door.

Soaked, she muttered nasty little French phrases to herself as she swiped raindrops from her cheeks and lips. She smoothed her wet hair, then held her arms out away from her body and shook the raindrops away like a peeved cat. Her hat, once a perky little thing, sagged limp over her brow. She fumed at it. He heard her and did not suppress his grimace.

At once she saw Clive, blinked, then did a little nod of acknowledgment. She patted her hat. Soaked, it dribbled water down her ears. She dashed the drops away and gave Clive a wide-eyed look that declared she was in control. But then, as she strode to the front desk, her shoes squished water.

"*Bon soir*, my lord," she said to Clive, then picked up the receptionist's bell and rang it.

"The rain drowned your hat," he offered quite reasonably, folding his hands before him.

"I'll salvage something from it for a new kite."

Clive snorted. "Save everything, do you?"

She locked her blue eyes on his, rueful and yet allowing in the humor of her cockeyed hat. "Everything worthwhile."

He let his own gaze offer his gratitude for what she had saved this morning. His voice rough with appreciation of her, he whispered, "But it's velvet. Will it fly?"

"If it does not fly, I'll make it sail."

Clive chuckled.

The receptionist appeared, a frown on his face from some issue he'd encountered in the back. However, his female guest smiled, clearly not in the mood for reciprocating his bad humor.

"Sir, *pardon*," she bade him with a smile. "Is the dining room still serving?"

"Yes, madam. Would you like a table?"

"No, I will order for my room."

"Allow me," Clive said, "to offer you my menu card."

"Bon soir, monsieur. Merci," she said as she took his menu and turned her serene gaze on Clive in appreciation. "I think you catch me always fresh from catastrophe!"

"It is my pleasure, madame." He beamed down at her, his fascination with the clear cerulean blue of her eyes making his knees weak. Was he fourteen? He gave a laugh. She took it as a response to her joke about her so-called catastrophe. All the while, he wanted to absorb her, sweep her up, hold her close, and take her to warmth, tea, blankets, and laughter.

What a delicate creature she was. She stood only as high as his shoulder. Her chin up, her cheeks wet with rain, tendrils of her hair hanging loose and dripping to her pelisse, she was the loveliest sprite he'd ever seen. So near her now, as he had not been this morning, he was also focused on the tiny details of her perfection. She was a picture any portraitist would want to paint. Fine of bone, pink of cheek, plump of lip, *my God*. For her looks alone, she was a woman any man could crave.

But he mustn't. He shook himself to polite discourse, but thought of not one appropriate word.

She read the menu, and he watched a drop of rain slide down her nape. He ground his teeth, the urge to kiss the back of her throat ringing through him like bells. He closed his eyes a minute to recover his sanity. But when he opened them, she was turning to him, and he knew she would say goodbye.

He could not have it. Not yet. Not while she was so damn wet and he was so wild to put his lips to her, to crush her against him as he had this morning. He grinned at that. He would like to catch her fresh, not only from the sea, but also from any storm—and yes, even fresh from her bath. *Rogue to think like that.* "Terrible weather to be out," he said like a simpleton. Anything to keep her with him.

"It came upon me in a rush," she said by explanation, even as she seemed to tear her gaze away from him.

Could she find him attractive? Dare he hope?

She returned to concentrate on the card and gave her dinner order to the clerk. Then she smiled up at Clive, curt and dismissive. "Forgive me, sir. I must retire."

He turned with her for the stairs—and his next words tumbled from his mouth. "You've had quite a day." He tried to sound jolly, offering her his arm to climb the staircase.

"Getting soaked twice?" She gave a small laugh. She changed her emotions as the situation called for it. At once reticent, the next instant allowing herself a moment of joy. Looping her arm through his, she lifted her wet skirts. "I'll try to catch more sun tomorrow to make up for it."

"As would I," he said, sounding to his own ears like some smitten schoolboy. *Bah!* What to say? "May Bella and I walk with you in the sun?"

Her doe eyes widened at first in joy, then in the negative. "I walk quickly. Bella could not keep up."

"We'd love to try, madame. Why not, eh? A little company, especially from those who have saved you from disaster, is a good thing."

She frowned in feigned dismay. "You are persistent, sir."

"My middle name," he affirmed with a nod. "Clive Persistent Davenport."

She threw back her head to chuckle—and it pleased him that he'd drawn her from her somber view of him. "I know the English. You love to name people, especially small boys with never-ending names. Tell me yours in its entirety."

"Ha! You have me out. Very well. Clive Allister Throckmorton Persistent Davenport."

"A mouthful."

"I don't use it all often."

"Wise." She knitted her brows. "I hope Bella is well."

"You change the subject." They reached the top of the stairs. He had little time to engage her for tomorrow.

"I do, sir. How is your daughter?"

"She is well, thank you. She remembers only your red kite and bothers me for one just like it. Did you buy it here in town? In the Lanes, perhaps?"

Delight transformed her face from beautiful to stunning. "Oh, monsieur, please allow me, s'il vous plaît, to make one for her." The offer was spontaneous and from a gladdened heart.

Enchantment spread through Clive like good red wine. "That's very kind of you, madame. Bella would welcome it."

At the door to her room, they paused.

"Merci beaucoup, Monsieur le…" She tipped her head. "Pardon, I do not know your rank, sir."

"Marquess." He downplayed the formalities of his position, but he held with them. "Marquess of Carlisle."

"Ah, mai oui. Which generation?"

"The eighth." He pursed his lips. Was she building a case that he was too lofty for her?

"The eighth *Marquis de Carlisle*," she said. "A gentleman, then, of very high esteem. Monsieur le marquis, an honor to meet you." A hand out in courtly form, she gave him a grand bow of homage. But her smile was full of a lighter mood than when he'd found her in the foyer. "Tomorrow, shall we say at eleven, we can meet in the reception room and I will bring all we need to make a new kite?"

He was to meet with Lord Langley in the garden of the Prince's Pavilion at one. "This will be wonderful. Bella will be very excited."

"May I call her Bella? That is, if you will allow me to address her by her given name."

"But of course." He chuckled, reluctant to let her go, though she must to dry off. "She calls herself Belle, so don't be surprised."

"Charming. I will remember. See you at eleven."

"At eleven."

She swept inside, and with a final smile from those rosebud-pink lips, she closed her door upon him.

He stood a moment, mesmerized by her petite beauty and good humor. Then he sobered.

Who do you meet, Madame Laurant of the pretty blue eyes and abilities to make kites? More importantly, who are you that you go out without escort and stand in the rain alone at night unit you are drenched and risk your health?

Chapter Four

GISELLE SANK BACK against her door, inhaling quickly to calm herself.

Mad at herself for finding le Marquis de Carlisle thrilling and funny, she plucked off her hat and let it drop to the carpet. Ruined. Not even fit for scraps for kite decoration. She'd give it to the maid tomorrow to throw away. She hurried to her bedroom, picking at her wet pelisse, muttering to herself about Carlisle's good looks and how easily he had charmed her from her fears just now.

Surprise at that made her smile. Men did not charm her as a rule. She frowned, admitting to herself she was too jaded, too put off by the men who had shamed her or hurt her. Those like Carlisle who treated a lady as their equal were few. Those who treated a lady like a jewel to be protected were rarer. A vision of her tall, silver-haired father, so upright, so principled, and so loving of his family, sprang to mind. The curve of Carlisle's lips when he smiled, the crinkles at the corners of his eyes, recalled the same of her father. Even his humor sparked the remembrance of her sire's.

But she should not compare Carlisle to her father. She hardly knew the marquis. He could be a card sharp, a gambler, a drunk. Worse, like her husband, he could be an arrogant sort who sought to dominate women. He could frequent whore-houses...though something about the way he took her in so openly told her he was no lecher, no man of ill repute.

Be done with this, Giselle! She shook him from her thoughts as she hung her pelisse on a chair back. It too might have to go. She fingered the coins in the tiny hem of the inside pocket. She'd extract those, if the coat were not salvageable.

Then she pushed down the bodice of her gown. The hem was torn and muddy. No repairing that. She'd dig out her coins she'd sewn into that hem and throw the gown away tomorrow, too. Then order another gown of midnight blue with red ribbons at the bodice and sleeves.

Carlisle had glimpsed the gown beneath her coat and admired the blue and red, just as he had liked her pink-and-lavender gown of this morning. He'd not said a word, but then—she grinned—he did not have to. *Argh!* She needed no man's approval.

In a rush, she worked at her petticoat, then her chemise. What would a man like Carlisle think of a lady who could not wait to be naked? Who disliked the attentions of maids? Who wanted buttons down the front of her gowns so that she could remove her clothes by herself? Even do without corsets? *As I do most days. Even tonight.*

Had he noticed?

No. Not tonight. Her bodice he could not see. But this after-noon, he definitely had when she was soaked, head to toe. From what he did not see tonight, he would assume she wore those hideous contraptions, like every other woman. Modesty demanded it, if health and vigor required a bit of lifting up, correct? Her breasts were sturdy, upright, pointed little things. In her gowns, she appeared well formed. Even generously so. Without stays to pull her up and out.

Did le Marquis de Carlisle like women with heavy breasts?

She arched her back. The instinct to compete had her chuck-ling. *Oh, now you are a naughty cat, Giselle Laurant!*

What was wrong with her? She stood on one foot and removed one half boot, then hopped about to take off the other. Stockings, too. She pushed her boots toward the floor of the cupboard and took her socks to drop them in a hamper.

There! She caught a glimpse of herself in the cheval glass. At twenty-six, she was not so badly formed. Petite, she had always been shorter than most other girls. She'd even noticed how far up she had to tilt her head to fully admire the beauty of this marvelous man Carlisle. Her breasts, if smaller than many, stood high. Her nipples, dark rose from her year of nursing her daughter, were large—and yes, erect. Pointed. Thinking of the luscious marquis did this to her.

She did not want to be lured by a man. Nor have a liaison with a marquis. Still, his looks were unusual. His magnetism, inescapable. Usually she saw men for what they were. The honorable, those who kept to their legacies, their estates, and most often their morals, she saw in the shades of blue and purples. The rest she saw in ruby reds as adventurers, bullies, frauds. Struck by the colors of those with whom she crossed paths, she had never been truly entranced with a man before. Let alone a stranger. A tall, gorgeous man whom she was shocked to say she saw in shades of silver and gold.

She shot a hand across her eyes. She had to stop this obsession. She had too many problems to be preoccupied with a man. A dashing cavalier. A gentleman with a child, a family, and a title far above that of the youngest daughter of the Vicomte de Touraine.

Agh! She padded to her clothes press and took out her night rail. Her negligee. A sinuous thing of creamy Lyon silk that she'd pampered herself to buy just before she left Paris, she pulled it over her head. Cold still, she shook out the matching robe lined in fuchsia satin. Better yet, she strode naked to the pile of bath linens and wound a towel around her wet hair.

She cast the tempting marquis from her midst, then climbed up into her delicious bed piled with blankets of wool and an ivory crocheted coverlet. Tomorrow, she had work to do. Her new drawing of Brighton was not finished. Glad the man who was to have rendezvoused with her tonight did not show, she criticized herself aloud that she was behind in her schedule. For now, she did not worry why he had not appeared. Tomorrow, he might send word somehow and be secretive about it. Meanwhile, she should be on to the next drawing.

She punched her pillow into the shape she liked and sighed into the soft bed. Yes, she thought of Carlisle. Persistent man! *Here again, monsieur le marquis?*

She knew how to banish him. Quickly, too. She best get to it.

Throwing the bedding aside, she strolled into her sitting room in search of her bottle of French cognac. She'd asked for cognac to be brought to her room the day before yesterday when she arrived. She enjoyed it, one glass each night, one of her small pleasures in her life alone. She poured, drank—and tonight, in honor of Monsieur le Marquis de Carlisle, she poured another good portion.

She closed her eyes and savored the smooth, hot fire of it down her throat. It warmed her…as the good looks of Carlisle did. Too bad she could not enjoy his interest in her. She'd not had a man in three years. She gave a bitter laugh as she went to her chaise longue and reclined. She had never had a man. Not really. Not totally. Her husband had had her. Ruthlessly, continuously, whenever he desired.

Her young girl's dreams to have a considerate husband had been dashed by his callousness. She had always counted herself fortunate that after a year of marriage and his nightly visits, she had gotten pregnant at last and put an end to his repeated, callous insults to her body. So too was she blessed that she had delivered her daughter in only nine hours. That her baby was in good health and perfect in form. That neither of them seemed to show the effects of her husband's heinous taste for chains and gags. Her midwife had never asked, if she had even noticed, that her body had been harshly invaded. Her husband only mated. Never had the man understood the art of making love. Giselle even doubted he had heard of the tenderness that could exist between a man and woman. Her parents had. Her brother and his wife had.

But she? No.

Another sip of the cognac sent hot ripples through her and a question formed loud in her head. Did the Marquis of Carlisle know how to take a woman and show her and him any joy?

Oh, stop. Just stop. You cannot care! You do not know that joy yourself…save for those two men you took to bed last year solely for the purpose of learning pleasure in the art of love. They had been congenial bed partners, but the momentary bliss they had brought her lacked the essential ingredient of love.

She must give off her thoughts of rapture and concentrate on her worries. They could fill her mind. Her own lack of progress on the first Brighton drawing. Now the added challenge that the man she had to deliver it to was not appearing at the time or place of their agreement.

Come to think of it, her personal guard had not appeared at all today. Not after noon. Not in her walking tour of the Steine park at four o'clock. She'd had not one glimpse of him today, and she usually had one each day. A reassurance, she supposed, that he took care of her. That he remained near. Yet he had not today. That, on top of the failure of Jacques Durand's man to appear tonight, had her considering a third pour of her cognac.

But no.

Durand's man had missed their first appointed meeting in Hastings weeks ago. He had appeared the next night. So she must not worry.

Just take care of your own responsibilities.

She would remain calm. Simple explanations always abounded. She'd wait patiently for Durand's agent. Perhaps tomorrow night he'd come.

And in the meantime, I'll not hunger for a man. For this marquis. After all, he is rich, titled, a perfect specimen of masculinity. Surely he is married. A man that appealing also certainly has a mistress. Or two.

Her heart fell to her feet. Oh, she would be so very disappointed if that were true. She much preferred him as she first beheld him, carefree, smiling, available, and—curse her own desires—obtainable.

But no. No and no.

I give one kite. For Bella. For myself, I take only that satisfaction.

From the delicious marquis, I accept the hot adulation of his gratitude.

That is all I shall do.

Then we part.

Chapter Five

BUT AT ELEVEN the next morning, Giselle sat in the main salon at a table filled with her supplies to make a kite. She had donned her newest gown, clothing the other indulgence beside cognac that she gave herself for her solitary life and the dangerous work she did. She glanced down at her skirts of a delicate muslin she called her summer cloud of blue. Telling herself she wore the pretty frock for confidence, she allowed herself the basic truth that the shade was an exact match for her eyes. Youthful silliness though it was, she'd taken longer than usual with her toilette this morning because she wished to impress monsieur le marquis. Fruitless as self-deception was, she did not usually lie to herself about anything, if she could help it. But this man lingered inside her, uplifting her, varied and bright as a rainbow.

He appeared no more than a minute later. He led by the hand his charming little girl.

Bella broke free from him and ran to her. "Madam"—she mangled the word, but Giselle did not care—"we make a kite. It will be red?"

"Exactly as the one we lost, Bella."

The child beamed at Giselle. Her heart twisted. She was so like her own Sophie, sprightly and fun, with her chubby cheeks and pink, heart-shaped mouth.

Giselle patted the chair beside her. "Come sit down."

"Bonjour, madame." The marquis was all smiles this morning. From his silver-gray waistcoat and apple-green frockcoat to his flashing gray eyes, the man mesmerized her. Nothing like her husband, who'd barely tolerated any act at any hour before two in the afternoon, this man seemed to have no bad humors. Only gaiety, love for his daughter, and smiles for both Bella and her.

He made her mouth water. She swallowed hard and killed the temptation to do more than greet him as a mere acquaintance.

"Do you mind if I sit with you?" He had his hand on the back of the chair next to Bella.

"Please do." At least he was far from her on the other side of his daughter. She turned her attentions to his child. "The important thing to remember about a kite is that it must be light as a feather." With a flourish, she produced a long white feather from the pocket of her skirt. Bella giggled as Giselle swept it down her little cheek. "Belle will fly. We shall make your kite so it flies very high."

The child went wide-eyed. "Wib feabbers?"

"The feathers are for you. But we'll make our kite so light that it seems to have them." Then Giselle pulled out four more, all of which she'd purchased from a milliner in the Lanes early this morning.

Bella took the five feathers and swiped them down her arm. "Tickles. Tickles," she sang to herself, and wiggled at the sensation.

Her father sat back, benevolent and approving.

"So, now," Giselle said to Bella, "we will start. We'll take these two sticks and put them together like that." She wound thin string around the jointure.

Bella picked up two more sticks and rubbed them together. The angle was not useful, and Giselle tried to change it.

But Bella frowned and shook her head. "No, no. This. This is..." She didn't finish the sentence but thrust her two sticks at

Giselle and nodded.

"Oui, *d'accord*," Giselle said, because she understood the demands of a child were often best not refused. "We will make your kite and another. How is that?"

Bella nodded eagerly.

"Madame," the marquis said in a warning tone as he turned to caution his daughter, "Bella knows she should follow your lead."

"Belle," blurted the little girl, "wants this kite."

"Yes, of course you do, sweetheart, but—"

Giselle reached out and put her hand atop his. The warmth, the firmness of him beneath her own flesh, made her stop and stare up into his large eyes. "We will make two," she said, though she had no idea where she found the logic of it. The man filled her head with visions of laughter and kisses. She tried to shake it all away...but the fires in her belly only flared higher.

He did not move, but his gaze devoured hers. "If you say so."

She nodded, suddenly tongue-tied.

He's married, titled, rich, and English. So far beyond you. So far above you, Giselle, that your desire for him has no future.

None.

Then a lady appeared on the threshold of the salon, called his name, strode to him—and bent to kiss his cheek.

"Ezz! Ezz!" Bella waved both her hands as she called to the lady.

"Hello, dumpling," the lady greeted her as she bussed the child's cheek and ruffled her blonde curls.

The marquis was on his feet, his arms around the woman. "I was so worried about you. What happened that you are so delayed?"

"The storm," she explained with a nonchalant tone. "We had to pause just outside Crawley for the night at an inn. Not a bad one, for the countryside, I must say."

Giselle got to her feet. This was his wife. His *wife*! She clutched her hands together. To be introduced to the marquise, she had to show respect for her betters. Manners did not die, even after guillotines did their worst.

"Well, I am relieved," he told the woman with a hug. "I was worried all night long."

"No need. Jamison knows our horses. Poor things had a devil of a night when that storm descended on us. He left ours in Crawley and paid to hire fresh ones for our journey here this morning. We'll get them when we return. Now," the woman said as she put her gloved hand to his forearm, "do introduce me to your charming friend."

"I will be delighted."

And he truly looked as though he was. That he should be so bold—and so out of character as to wish to make her acquainted with his wife—took Giselle's breath. Her heart shriveled like a child's deprived of candy.

"Terese, my dear, allow me to present Madame Laurant. Madame, Lady Winterton, my sister."

The news sang through Giselle's bones, so much so that she had her hand out to the woman. "I am pleased to meet you, my lady."

The marquis was grinning. "Madam Laurant has been so gracious as to help Bella construct a kite."

"How exciting," said the lady, winking at Bella.

"We had a mishap yesterday on the beach, and the kite Madame Laurant had made flew away."

"I see." She frowned, her soft gray eyes so like her brother's. "What kind of mishap?"

"Bella rushed to hold it and lost the lead. She fell into the sea just as a wave came for us all, and it was Madame Laurant who saved our Bella."

"Well!" The lady gazed at Giselle with fresh delight, that too so true and genuine like her brother's. "Thank you, madam. Our Bella can be impulsive, and I'm glad you were quick to act."

"As was I, my lady. I know how children of this age cannot understand the fullness of what they do."

Terese, or rather Lady Winterton, tipped her head. "You have a child of your own, madame?"

"Non. I did…but she is gone."

The woman reached out to take Giselle's hand. "I am so sorry. To lose a child is heartbreaking."

Giselle preferred not to talk about this. "It is. Very." She looked up into the face of the marquis. His expression had melted to compassion for her loss. Flustered, she said, "You both have much to discuss, so if you prefer, we can postpone our kite making until later."

"No, Clive," the lady objected, and touched his wrist. "I will settle myself in my room. Unpack. Order a service of tea and sandwiches. Terrible food in that inn, you know. Adieu, Madame Laurant. Thank you for saving our little girl. She is the light of our lives."

"I was happy to help, Lady Winterton." Giselle smiled as his given name resounded in her head. *Clive. Gentle Clive is simply a man, not a lofty marquis. Clive, friendly, kind, and chivalrous.* Giselle liked the color of his name. Gold, like him.

Lady Winterton twiddled her fingers at the three of them. "Do not rush, Clive. I need an hour or so to myself."

With that, she was off, and the marquis was left standing there gazing down at Giselle.

"Shall we continue with the kite?" he asked in a mellow tone. "I'd like to see it through. Bella would, too."

They both glanced over at the array of joined sticks that Bella had made.

Giselle, free of her fear that Terese was his wife and bemused by the mess Bella had made, beamed at this man whom she enjoyed more with each passing moment. "Well, goodness. Look at that. Hmmm. Bella, that's an intriguing shape." *Like a garden worm.*

He chuckled at her words and at the jumbled thing his daughter had made. Then he shocked her and took her hand in his. "Look at me. You were pleased to hear that Terese is my sister."

The surprise of his touch matched the jolt of his words. But she loved being held by him. "Did I reveal so much?" she ventured, and knew once her words were out, she should not have been so bold.

"You show me almost everything you are," he said beneath his breath. "I have no idea why that is."

Alarmed, she admitted to herself that she knew why. But to him, her answer was, "No, nor I."

"But I beg you not to change."

A man and woman entered the room.

Giselle went quite still. "Oh, sir, that is not wise."

"Tell me why."

She rolled a shoulder and tried to free her hand from his. He would not let her go. "I am French."

He arched a long, inquisitive golden brow. "Are you my enemy?"

"No." That was so true. "Never."

"I did not think so."

"Still, monsieur, you are a marquis."

"Does that make me ineligible to be your friend?"

"No, but—"

"Tell me why not, madame."

She stiffened her spine. "I am a foreigner in your land."

"Yet not so foreign that you are not permitted a license to visit the southern coast in this time of peril."

"That is true. I am quite harmless." *Except for the work I do.* Her friends who worked in London had obtained that license for her. No official had asked to see it yet. For that, Giselle was happy. She disliked feeling different...branded. Yet what she created was definitely a singular product. Proud of it, she assumed no one else had her abilities or her unique task. Or so it seemed. Out of curiosity these past months here in England, she had searched London's, Greenwich's, and Dover's book- and print shops for anything resembling her work. There was none. Only her older brother had accomplished the same sort of diagrams. For his audacity to show the real lay of estate lands along the Loire River, he had gone to La Force and died there. Those who owned large tracts of land and who had defrauded the government of tax money had joined together and deluded the government tax collectors, blaming her brother for fraud.

She stilled at the memory of his death. Now that he was gone, only she knew how to do this particular art.

To the marquis, she said, "I…I work for my living."

"So do I."

She put two fingers to her lips. His gaze followed and melted all her reserve. "You run an estate."

"Among other things," he replied.

She raised her face to the ceiling. She must warn him off. Frustrated he would not relent, she swallowed her dismay. "I am no one. I should remain so to you."

"That time when you could be no one to me has passed. You've saved my daughter from the sea. You've made her morning a happy one."

"Little doings, sir."

"Not to me. Nor her."

She snatched back her hand. "You have been gracious to me, sir."

He turned cool, narrowing icy gray eyes upon her. "Do you refuse to see me because you have a lover?"

"No! None!"

"I know you were to meet a man last night outside the hotel."

She sucked in a breath. *What to say about that?*

"And he left you waiting for him out in the rain, my dear." He took her hand once more. "Will you meet him and disappear with him?"

"No, no. It is not like that."

"Then he is…what to you?"

"Business." Oh, why had she admitted that? "Business!"

"I see." He relaxed, full of a rogue's confidence. "So I may call upon you without a contender for your affections."

"My affections, sir, are not to be had."

"No?" He gave her a pure, sweet smile.

She stiffened. "What will your wife say?"

"Nothing. She died two years ago."

Her mouth opened.

"I am free, madame, to court you honorably. Did you think I would do so otherwise?"

"No, I see who you are. All of you. Noble and wise. How can I do that? I do not know you. I do not."

"Nor do I know all of you, my dear. But you stir me. I gaze at you and find new vistas I wish to explore."

"You mustn't. I am a widow, sir. Alone in your country. My family—my husband and daughter, my brother, my sister and parents—are gone. Life has not been easy and I...I have few affections left."

He brought her hand to his lips and pressed an angel's kiss to her fingertips. "Allow me to help you find your lost affections. I confess I have a few of my own I must reclaim."

His words swept her along as if she took to the sky with him.

"Let us finish these two kites. Then go out into the air and send them up where we will wish we, too, could fly with gay abandon."

Oh, he had a subtle art with words that warmed her blood with hot, red longing. "Yes. I want that."

"Good." He tucked her hand between both of his. "I am in earnest, dear madame. We will declare we aid each other in some kind of rehabilitation. To find great joy is a treasure to which few devote themselves. Let us do it, shall we?"

$$\text{Chapter Six}$$

"**S**HE IS LOVELY." Terese raised her teacup to her smiling lips. Clive cast her a withering look as he buttoned his frockcoat.

"It's been two years since Christine died. You've mourned her death."

He shook his head. More like he'd mourned his failures with her.

"So many ladies are eager to become your new wife."

"I'm not looking for a new one." He fumbled with his cravat, grousing to himself that he should have brought his valet with him to Brighton.

She gave him a broad grin. "It appears you don't have to."

"Terese," he pleaded with her, "stop." Madame Laurant was indeed the only one who appealed to him. All of her drew him. Her fresh face, her delicate form, her large, almond-shaped blue eyes as she took him in and caressed him with a yearning he wagered she did not perceive. They had flown kites with Bella for more than an hour—and he could have sworn his heart flew up to frolic with the two little red birds.

Bella had marveled and chuckled, then worn herself out. She was abed, napping from her carefree morning in the sun. He did not have to nap. The memory of that hour still lived within him.

It would, he knew, for days or more to come.

When have you known unfettered delight like that with a woman?

Not even when he had courted his wife had he thought he could grab such simple pleasures. No kite flying then. Only quiet picnics. Boring balls. And walks among gardens where conversations were stilted and filled with gossip of the *ton*.

His sister was still talking, and he stared at her.

"You have not heard a thing I said, have you?" Terese feigned horror.

"I do apologize."

She flicked a hand and laughed. "Clive, I'd like to see you happy with a woman. Truly happy."

He gave Terese a sidelong glance. He should be careful with his heart and with Madame Laurant's. "You are assuming a lot from a five-minute introduction."

"Sometimes that is all one needs. Ah, I am right, then," she crooned, and fluttered her long brown lashes. "Lightning can strike in mere minutes."

"All right." He plunked his hands on his hips. *How do you know?* was the question that sprang to his lips. But he did not want her to describe his enchantment. He felt what it was. He did not need a recitation of what he looked like. He resembled a clown in harlequin or that proverbial besotted schoolboy who hankered after the upstairs maid. "I must go. Langley will wonder what detains me."

"I will read and nap. Take your time with your meeting. When Bella awakens, she and I will have tea and sandwiches in the dining room. Then I will ask her to show me how to fly that kite she made."

He waggled his brows at that. "A trick if it goes again." Madame Laurant had flown Bella's odd little worm of a kite. How she got it up was a mystery, but the contraption flew for at least ten minutes. He'd been the one to maneuver madame's kite. Of course, the darn thing flew like a bird. While Bella had jumped for joy that both flew, the shared laughter between madame and himself made for a delicious torment. "I wish you luck."

"Madame Laurant did a fine job of fixing Bella's creation," Terese said with wicked glee in her gray eyes. "The lady knows how to please a child. I'd say a man as well, eh?"

"You never let go of a bone, do you?"

"My specialty, darling. Go! Meet Langley. Give him my regards."

"I will. Do you see him soon?"

"Here? I do hope so. Now leave me!"

Clive waved himself off. At reception, the clerk asked if he needed a carriage, but no, he needed to walk. Terese, older by two years, knew him well, and she had pricked his memory. Reflection on the past was not a favored pastime. Nor was instant enchantment with a lady he did not know his usual practice. He was so careful. Even to choose a mistress. Even then, he'd pensioned his latest one off last autumn. Boredom was a terrible calamity in bed.

Was his problem that he was too careful?

Or had fate just played an ironic joke on him? *See a lady. Love her looks. Find her once more. Appreciate her kindness, her spontaneity, her reserve. Enjoy her. Ponder why you must not pursue her or have her.* Yet his body tingled with the promise of desire.

Such an odd feeling, desire. It came without logic. Dropped before one like the vow of a new world. Pulled one inside and lingered, tested, and teased. And it was all fantasy.

Oh hell. End this!

At a snap, he took the lane up to the Regent's Pavilion. The sun was murderously bright, hot for June, and his mind went to the matter he would discuss with the Earl of Langley and the prime minister's aide.

He cocked his ear. A military band played a ditty and the boisterous sound came steadily toward him. People in the street paused to listen and look from what direction they came. Preston Barracks lay barely two miles north of Brighton, housing artillery and cavalry as well as hundreds of horses in the stables. Their complement had doubled in the past three months.

With Boney's *La Grande Armée* camped directly across the Channel in Boulogne, British defenses along the southern coast had more than doubled. Soldiers, sailors, cannon, and lorries filled with new rifles and uniforms and God knew what else filled the streets every hour of the day. If the French came across the Channel, Clive had intelligence that they'd most likely come by boat at night. Boney, said Clive's own agent here in town, repeated that he wanted to cross by hot air balloon. But Clive and Langley, as well as their colleagues in espionage, knew the emperor's idea was literally full of air.

Still, manpower along the Kent and Sussex shoreline was not up to that of Dover and Hastings. Staffed by volunteers, the bulk of the defense here—actually twice the number of men stationed at Preston—was civilian home guard. Insufficient to the task of proper defense, they were mostly untrained. Many were without rifles, pistols, or even a slingshot. The truth was that if Boney came, his disciplined, well-armed soldiers would overwhelm the small coastal towns. In the blink of an eye, one twelve-hour stint, Britain would be French.

Three army officers strode around him. The two young ladies who approached them tittered to each other. They appeared to be inviting contact. When the girls preened and batted their lashes, the officers tipped their hats but did not stop—and the girls complained to each other as they passed by Clive.

He muttered to himself of his own frustrations as he took a turn into the gardens of the pavilion.

"I say, old man, you look gloomy!" The Earl of Langley rose from the bench outside the door of the regent's favorite home and strode toward him. About twenty years older than Clive, Langley was a tall, lean, platinum-haired fellow with easy grace. He worked for the Foreign Office when he was not attending to his estate, his four brothers, their wives, and their dozen or so offspring. He was devoted to his wider family, but most especially to his eight-year-old son. A widower, Langley had not had a happy marriage. He and Clive had often spoken about how readily young men could marry mistaking lust for love. "What is your problem?"

"Not sure I know! Hello, how are you?"

They shook hands.

"Very well. Shall we go in," Langley asked, "or prepare here before we go inside?"

"Here, yes." Clive sat down. "I need to apply my mind to this matter before us."

"That bad, is it? What ails you? I know you have no problems with money."

"Never. My father did well by the tenants, and my estate manager is finer than I could ever be."

"Your sister then?" Langley frowned, very concerned.

"No. She's perfect."

Langley nodded. "Good. Glad to hear it. Tell her I said that, will you?" Langley had come to a dinner party at Clive's London house a few weeks ago. He had met her the year Terese debuted, but she was soon to become engaged, and Langley was married. Their interest in each other was polite, even if a spark had burned from then on.

Now both had lost their spouses. When Langley took Terese in to dinner that night at Clive's, their interest in each other blossomed. Langley had called two or three times a week to take Terese for carriage rides. Terese had invited him to her recent garden party. Clive had been pleased when Terese agreed to come on this holiday with him and Bella. But he suspected she knew Langley would be in town, too.

"Terese sends her regards." His sister had married an older man by order of their father, but she had found love with him and, unlike the earl, enjoyed the bliss of it. Yet her happiness had been short. Her husband died of an intestinal disease years ago. Terese had found solace in caring for Bella...and in monitoring Clive's own despair after his wife's death. She knew, as no others did, that he did not mourn Christine's loss as greatly as he regretted that the two of them had never found any mutual satisfaction in their union.

"I will call upon Terese at the hotel," Langley said. "Tomorrow, perhaps?"

"She will welcome that."

Langley looked pensive. "You don't mind, do you, that I call on her?"

"Dear heavens, no! Why would I?"

"I am so much older."

"Doddering, are you?"

"I'm fifty-two, Carlisle. How old is Terese?"

"Thirty-seven. But how can age matter more than a meeting of minds? Or the comfort of shared outlooks?" *How indeed!*

Langley ran a hand through his silver-streaked hair. "Did I say those very words to you last week?"

Clive chuckled and took a look around to ensure he would not be overheard. "When you and I spoke about lust?"

Langley rolled his eyes and laughed. "Yes."

"Bah! Call on my sister, Langley. She enjoys your company. She is a good woman, and she misses a good man in her life."

"Thank you. May I take that as approval if I ask her for her hand?"

"My heartiest approval, sir. Tarry not a day, will you?"

"I should go see her tonight, then."

"Do it. Join us for dinner, why don't you?"

"I will."

They took another turn around the path toward the door.

Langley asked, "What, then, bothers you?"

Clive extended a hand. The failure of his marriage shrouded his thinking. "Let's walk about the garden, eh?"

"A woman." Langley grinned.

"Am I transparent?"

"Evidently to me, yes."

"To my sister, as well."

Langley threw back his head to laugh. "Then I'd say you

definitely have a romantic problem."

"Please. I am too old for that."

"Didn't you just tell me age is no limit on love?"

Clive had to take his colleague to task—and did so with a smile. "You have me there."

His friend shrugged. "I have the same problem as you. Terrible first marriage. Reluctant to face shackles again."

"It's a bad trick to play on a man or woman. Show them an irresistible someone and always, always, give them some barrier, some crisis of mind that the two of you cannot be happy after the first five times in bed."

Langley stopped in his tracks. "You are in bad straits." He opened, then snapped shut, his pocket watch. "Our friend awaits us inside."

"Good. Let's tackle a problem that can be solved."

Langley frowned over that. "I'm glad to hear you say so. Since we met last week, Mulgrave has new evidence of another double agent."

"What a tangle." Clive shook his head. Foreign Secretary Henry Phipps, Baron Mulgrave, was new in his post, appointed by Prime Minister Pitt only in January. His charge, along with the home secretary's, was to protect Britain from Boney's invasion. Formerly a general in His Majesty's Army, Mulgrave had many supporters who claimed he knew how to fortify from within and without. "Has he any information from his agents in Paris?"

"Two of them were arrested by Fouché's man, René Vaillancourt, last week. The third made it to Le Havre by the skin of their teeth. The newest word from him is that we have a nest of double agents along the Channel coast. Women who pass information to other women."

"At garden parties. Or at tea."

"Exactly." Langley shook his head. "Mulgrave's upset with our lack of progress."

Clive's stomach turned. "He has reason to be."

"You've not found the source of those odd diagrams of Hastings, I take it?"

"Not yet." Clive had visited a friend of his in Hastings four weeks ago. His friend, a retired navy man, had written to Clive about a series of three sketches of the shoreline of Hastings that his wife had found in a bookstore. She had thought it odd that the drawings were folded and left inside a book of poetry for sale upon the shelf.

"But stranger still was the fact that all of the renderings were incorrect. In one pencil sketch, the shoreline was distorted and the buildings dotting the coast incorrectly sized. Another ink drawing, unique in its aerial view of the town, attempted to define the shoreline from above the buildings. The third drawing was a haphazard painting done in watercolors and the shoreline was also incorrect."

Clive sighed. "Whoever was to have bought that book of poetry has not appeared to buy it. I had a good discussion with the owner, and put two men to watch the shop, but no one who has come recently has asked for that particular book. As of last week, my friend wrote to inform me that it still sits upon the shelf."

"You put the drawings back in the book?"

"I did. The owner of the shop writes every day to tell me about its fate. I fear that in the time during which my friends had the drawings in their possession, someone came to buy that book. We may have missed the connection."

A roar of men's wild shouts carried on the afternoon breeze.

Langley cast his gaze to the sky. "The Grand Army?"

Clive widened his eyes at the sound of more than two hundred thousand French so dangerously near. "Giving us hell from their camp in the plains of Boulogne, holding maneuvers. Perhaps even our good friend Bonaparte is there today to give out more prizes for his new Legion of Honor."

"GOOD MORNING TO both of you!" Lord Halsey strode toward them as Langley opened the door to the pavilion. Halsey daily reported to his very good friend, the prime minister, any new information about the French navy's maneuvers in the Atlantic Ocean. "Glad I caught you. Feared I'd be late."

"Never!" Clive put out his hand to the PM's advisor.

Langley offered his own welcome.

Inside the foyer, Clive was amused by the bright yellows and greens of the Chinoiserie décor. The prince regent had created a Mughal palace in architecture outside, but inside, a Chinese display of colorful porcelains and paintings dazzled the eye.

Clive stopped, shocked at his next thought. Giselle would love to see this array of color and style.

"Let's go up." He recalled his purpose here and nodded toward the staircase. "The prince's steward has set aside a room for us to meet."

"I'm eager," Halsey said as they took the stairs, "to hear your latest news, Carlisle. Your agent in Boulogne does such good work." Halsey had come down from London to Brighton just to meet with Clive, who had written that he had new intelligence from his man in Boulogne. His man had arrived day before yesterday with his latest. He told Clive that the French navy were preparing to cross the Channel any day.

No one was on the stairs with them, and Clive was tempted to speak freely, but did not. "Let's go to our room, shall we?"

Inside, Clive shut the door and did not sit, but faced his two friends. "My man has seen those amphibious landing barges the French navy wants to use to come ashore here."

"Are they as effective as the Royal Navy thinks?" Halsey still stood, eager to hear Clive's news.

Clive let a grin overtake him. "Their landing flaps that dip down into the sea so soldiers can easily disembark and run ashore are so low, men must swim out."

"With their weapons in hand?" Halsey asked.

"Rifles at the ready." Clive arched a brow. "But the first out drown."

Langley tsked.

"How unfortunate," Halsey said with a smile.

"Worse, their floating gunships with twelve cannons have defective gun turrets."

"How so?" Langley was aghast.

"The whole boat has to be pointed toward the target. Tough to do on choppy Channel waters."

"You have details, I hope?" Halsey pressed.

Clive was beside himself with glee. "Many."

Chapter Seven

GISELLE TOOK THE back servant stairs at a clip and left the hotel in the basement through the kitchen door. This morning, she'd told herself she had no need to be fancy to complete her errands and buy a new supply of watercolors. She'd strolled outside the hotel earlier this morning and felt the humid air. She had donned an older gown of apple green with a matching shawl. To top it off, she had chosen a plain cloche straw hat that hid her features.

Pausing on the walkway, she glanced about. The streets were empty of foot traffic. Only a few public carriages and lorries crisscrossed, out and about at this early hour. No one suddenly appeared. Not even her regular guard—again. She had strolled the shore briefly yesterday to take her measurements and had not spotted hide nor hair of him.

She had seen Lord Carlisle. Not to talk to. But both days, she had emerged from her rooms to walk the town and do her calculations. Tuesday, she'd spied him with Bella and his sister, enjoying ices in a small café. Yesterday, they ran the two kites Giselle and Bella had constructed Monday.

Giselle had not approached them. They looked so carefree, she did not want to intrude on their fun. Yet she was pleased he had not yet returned home, wherever that was. That meant, hope against hope, vain as that was, that they might meet again.

As for her guard, who knew where he was? He seemed to have vanished. Disturbed by his absence, she tempered her anxiety by focusing on her exact measurements of height, distance, and quality. Then she had returned to her rooms to put all her knowledge to her primary pencil sketches.

But in one way or another, both men hampered her progress with her work. If she could not go out with absolute confidence in her safety, venture about the town at will, how could she complete her sketches and watercolors on time? She had already missed one deadline for the seascape of Ramsgate. That, she would have to skip. She was not going back. The drawings of Brighton would complete the set of townscapes she'd been ordered to produce. Ramsgate—her friend and coordinator Lady Ashley had told her—would most likely not be a choice for the French to land. She would not worry about it.

But she did grumble to herself about men and duty. "Yet do not complain." Only with Ramsgate, and now here in Brighton, had she encountered problems. In Ramsgate, it was bad weather that had deterred her daily research trips. Here in Brighton, she seemed to have lost her bodyguard. His lack annoyed her, but she resolved that it would not constrain her. She went about town anyway.

She stopped to gaze into a modiste's shop window. A bolt of royal-purple silk rippled across the floor of the display. She licked her lower lip, seeing herself in a ball gown that flowed around her like a royal river as she danced with monsieur le marquis. Clive. *Dear Clive.*

Bah! Non! *Fantasy!*

Still, she wanted that gorgeous silk. Plus, the dressmaker, she could tell by the fine stitching on the yellow dress in the corner of the window, offered excellent craftsmanship. She began to turn toward the shop entrance. But a frisson whirled through her. She paused. Reflected in the wide window, a man stood against a lamppost across the street. He was long, lean, beak nosed, and beady eyed. In truth, he resembled a man she'd seen briefly when she was in Hastings. His gaze slid over her in a deathly stare, then he shifted and walked in the opposite direction. The hair on her neck tingled now as it had then in Hastings.

Her next thought disturbed her in a different way. Months ago, when she had rented a small cottage along the Thames in Richmond, she'd felt the same phenomenon, as if…as if someone watched her. The feeling had been oddly pleasant. Her intuition told her she should not be afraid of that experience. Days later, when she had spied a tall, blond, handsome man in town, she imagined it might be he who observed her. She'd shaken off that illogical assumption, and indeed, she'd not felt that way since leaving Richmond. She had become watchful then, but had never felt afflicted. Nor had she discovered anyone near her. She'd forgotten that until now.

She sucked in a huge breath and pushed her fears away. She went inside the shop and stood for the measurements for a glorious purple silk gown. It would be a devastatingly gorgeous creation, frivolous of her to commission, but she'd have it. She deserved her small rewards. Her mind full of her work, she allowed herself a smile. Tomorrow she'd meet her two friends from London, Lady Ashley and Lady Ramsey, who came to Brighton to discuss her progress. She would tell them about the laxness of her guard…and that man there who seemed familiar.

The only way to test if he were following her was to hurry on now to do her errands. If he wished to cause mischief, he could not possibly think of advancing on her in broad daylight. Besides, Gus and Amber—Lady Ashley and Lady Ramsey—would see her safe and secure.

Out of the modiste's, she bought her supplies in the Lanes and hurried back to her rooms. There she settled in, submerged herself in her work…and forgot about the draw of sun and sea and salty air.

But that was not an easy feat.

She laughed and put down her pencil. It should be easy to

crush her need to laugh and play with little Bella Davenport.

And forget the beguiling Lord Carlisle.

But it was not.

CLIVE ROSE FROM the table outside the sweet shop. Langley must have some emergency with his contact. Their plan, should one be unable to meet, was to do so the following day. Same time, same place.

He could wait. His agent out of Broadstairs had failed to post. So Clive had no news for his friend and colleague.

"Lord Carlisle?" A lady stepped before him. "How lovely to see you here."

Amber duClare, Lady Ramsey, extended her hand in greeting. A gorgeous creature with sizzling red hair and snapping green eyes, she and her friend Augustine Whittington, Lady Ashley, were noted society hostesses.

"My lady," he said as he took her hand. "You make my day sunnier."

"Charmer," she teased him, and cocked a brow. "Have you met my friend, Lady Ashley? My dear," she said, and turned to the young woman beside her, "allow me to present Lord Carlisle, Clive Davenport."

The dark-haired beauty was smiling. "I have often heard of your work in the Lords for voting reforms, sir. I am honored to meet you."

"As am I to formally meet you. Have you ladies a desire for the crumpets?" Both ladies were friends, Clive had long known. Married to men who were not only friends themselves, but colleagues, so said rumor. Clive had met Lady Ramsey only a few weeks ago in London at a reception at the Russian embassy. There he'd also exchanged a few words with her husband, said to be an agent, as was his wife, for the famous city merchant Scarlett

Hawthorne.

The Scarlett ring was unofficial and frowned upon by the home and foreign secretaries. The prime minister could not confirm Scarlett's agents' success with any hard evidence, nor with any regularity. A problem of merchant trade and agents' lack of temperance, he termed it. Yet he valued Scarlett's work when he could confirm its accuracy. He declared that the government needed all the help they could get to smother the bastard, Napoleon. Bound as the PM was by what he knew and what he wished he could learn, he often decreed that a secret was only that if two people knew it. He chided his official ministers to live up to the reported rumors of the lady merchant's smart network. She sat in the City in Clements Lane, but her elegant fingertips controlled strings on innumerable agents that reached as far as Cairo, Jappa, Athens, and, said some, perhaps even the ruthlessly ruled kingdoms of Tripoli and the tribes of Africa who miraculously escaped the horror of the sub-Sahara slave trade.

Clive smiled and tipped his hat to the two ladies. "I do recommend everything here, however."

"You are leaving?" Lady Ramsey's eyes swept over his empty plate and cup and saucer.

"I am." He made to go.

"We could sit, couldn't we, Gus, and become better acquainted?"

"I apologize, but I must leave." He wished to heaven he could stay and learn what he could about why they were here in town, if indeed there was a reason other than the pleasure of the moment. "I have another appointment, you see."

"A shame. Well!" Lady Ramsey said with a bright smile. "My husband and I host a ball in the grand salon of the Old Ship Hotel three evenings' hence. Please come. I will send round a proper invitation. Where do you lodge?"

He grinned. "The Old Ship."

"There you have it!" She beamed. "You can simply run down the stairs. I know Godfrey would love to get to know you better."

"And my husband, Lord Ashley, would as well," Lady Ashley added.

Because the foreign secretary had long wished that his own agents would coordinate espionage activities with those of Scarlett Hawthorne, Clive thought it the perfect opportunity to draw closer to a few. "Thank you, I would like that myself. I will be delighted to attend."

He was making to leave them with a nod when Madame Giselle Laurant turned the corner of the bakery shop and halted at sight of the two ladies with him.

Her eyelashes flickered, the only sign of her distress. Her gaze on the two women, she proceeded to walk backward out of sight.

What was wrong?

He bade both ladies good day and took the lane straight before him. As he passed the corner into which madame had retreated, he noted from the corner of his eye that she had disappeared.

The obvious answer was that she knew Lady Ramsey and/or Lady Ashley, and did not wish to speak with them.

Why? What was her fear of being discovered by those two ladies?

He hurried back to his rooms. He had a report to write for Foreign Secretary Mulgrave.

His questions about Madame Laurant had to wait until later. Better yet, this business in the Lanes warned that he should forget her.

But recent attempts throughout his days and nights said that was not so.

GISELLE SANK INTO the hollow crevice behind the corner of two shops. That had been close to disaster. She had covered her shock at Gus and Amber's early arrival in town, and properly so.

Had she continued and approached them, Lord Carlisle would have seen by Amber and Gus's reactions to her that they and she were acquainted. Both ladies were expert at discretion, but Giselle wished not to navigate the murky waters of espionage in the presence of Carlisle. The less he knew about her, the better.

Three years ago, each of the two ladies had met the men to whom they were now married. Agents for a network of spies managed here in London by a lady merchant, both Lords Ashley and Ramsey had left France after the declaration of war and brought their lady loves with them here to England's shores.

Giselle had not seen either lady since they had met in Paris until she'd arrived in England last autumn. That journey from her home near Blois, along the Loire River, had been long and dangerous. Only with the help of one of Ashley's men—his former majordomo of his house in Paris—had she been able to make secret connections to get to Le Havre on the coast. Not only was she escaping from Joseph Fouché's deputy, René Vaillancourt, but she was gifted with a rare talent. Amber and Gus knew that skill could help the British cause. They and their husbands had welcomed her to England, smuggled in as she was by one of their colleagues. Jacques Durand, by name. It was Durand's associate who had not posted a few nights ago outside the hotel.

She winced. She had too much on her mind to play the polite lady who met old friends on the street. Never had she been a good actress. It was her frankness, her lack of subterfuge, that had created the tensions with her husband. But it was on her ability to truly see people for what they were that she had built her strength and survived her husband's cruelty and his embezzlement of public tax money. The French deputy had argued that to scrub the public records of her husband's theft, she could become Vaillancourt's mistress. She knew it a false and vengeful offer. Vaillancourt had loved only Amber St. Antoine, now Lady Ramsey. His loss of her to Ramsey in a scene that denigrated Vaillancourt publicly sparked that man's resentment of Amber and all her friends. Giselle's alternative, he said, was to be shackled and go to the infamous Parisian prison of La Force. Long ago with the death of her husband by Vaillancourt's order, Giselle had vowed never to allow another man to mistreat or abuse her.

She summoned now the pride that she had escaped Vaillancourt's threats and concentrated on her future. She turned and walked back at a brisk pace. She'd return to the Lanes tomorrow for her supplies. Three days' hence she would meet her two friends in the house they had rented here. That had been the plan for the three of them to meet. Gus, Lady Ashley, had sent a letter to her at the hotel last week confirming that. Clearly, they had changed their plans unexpectedly and arrived earlier.

Giselle hurried along, calming herself. There had been no mishap. She was fine, saved from a tense scene. She intended to live a very long time in serenity. Rewarding herself was her way to calm her nerves and grant herself those little prizes that made her life enjoyable.

So as reward, when she returned, she would sketch for herself a new gown or two, serviceable styles to replace those so recently ruined by the sea and the rain. She would also sketch a new embroidery design for a bodice. Or perhaps for the cover of a new reticule—and take them all to the modiste in the Lanes who created her new royal-purple silk gown. She deserved nice things. Beautiful things. She'd have them…and once her work here was done, she might even allow herself a true holiday. She'd go, perhaps, to Cornwall. There, she'd heard, were dramatic coasts and landscapes in that far corner of England to rival those on the French Normandy coast near Étretat.

She could live as she wished—and immediately a vision of Carlisle stood before her. Tall, bold, laughing, he could be in her life after this task of hers was finished. He could be hers in the fullness of time. She saw the interest in the sparkling depths of his silver-gray eyes. She could have him, perhaps not forever but for a day, a week, an interlude filled with rapture.

But no. *No!* She was not for him. She was not a virginal lady with a pristine past and only a spotless future before her. Still, she closed her eyes. She could imagine him without all the folderol of his cravat and this and that and other. Naked to her eye and her hand, he would be a marvel in bed. Inventive and tender, he would fulfill her one desire for bliss she'd barely glimpsed. He would be a man she could savor for as long as he wished, for as long as she cared to amuse him.

Oh, she was quite mad for him, wasn't she?

She sped along. She was fantasizing now. *Crazy, you are, Madame Laurant.*

She chuckled at herself and slowed. She picked another dream. Achievable, too. She could live in Cornwall for a long time, find a man who appealed. She would be picky. Choose a nice man. A kind man. Someone who resembled one dashing marquis she was beginning to suspect she would never forget.

But was there anyone his equal?

No. Do not fool yourself, Giselle.

There is no one.

Chapter Eight

A S SOON AS Giselle closed her door the next morning on the footman who'd brought her breakfast, she strode to her table to open the two surprise letters on the tray. One was on Amber's stationery, and she begged Giselle to forgive the delay in notifying her that she and Gus had arrived early in town. But their husbands had business to conduct and they all came posthaste. Amber also told her to open the other letter on her tray if she had not already. The second note was paper of a delicate ivory, scented with lemon verbena, and Giselle knew at once whose it was. Tickled as a child that the letter most likely came from one of her mother's best friends, Giselle tore it open.

Oui, miraculous! Madame Élisabeth-Louise Vigée-Le Brun, the famous portraitist of Marie Antoinette and so many other royals and dignitaries, not only currently visited Brighton, but she invited Giselle to luncheon tomorrow.

Giselle had had no idea the famous portrait painter was here in town. Furthermore, the lady had discovered she too was in Brighton. How that had occurred was no mystery. The answer had to be that her friends, Amber and Gus, had sent word to Madame Le Brun that Giselle was here in Brighton. Amber and Gus not only knew the famous portraitist from their years in France, but also that Giselle had known the artist had been one of her mother's good friends. The Frenchwoman knew that Giselle would not refuse her invitation.

Giselle sat with a smile and sigh, her reverie providing glimpses of her childhood. She remembered well her mother's and the lady's laughter in each other's company. In her family's Paris house in the Rue du Bac, Giselle had studied madame's work as she painted portraits of her parents. Later, the artist had come to their chateau on the Loire and painted one landscape of their verdant forest along the rushing river. Taken by her mother to view Le Brun's studio in Paris, Giselle fell in love with the ability to produce not only landscapes true to a leafy tree, but creations of others' faces in hues and shades so real that the people could step off the canvas into the world.

Giselle had not seen Madame Le Brun in many years. The lady had fled Paris and traveled over much of the Continent since the royal Bourbons had been guillotined twelve years ago. Her visits to any notable man or woman in any part of the world were duly reported by newspapers everywhere. She made her way among the titled, rich, and famous, many of whom she had met when she was the favored artist and portraitist of Queen Marie Antoinette.

Giselle had endeavored to be as good, though she knew her skills at painting people would never equal madame's. She stuck to scenery, landscapes, and seascapes, and called herself useful, if never brilliant.

That Madame Le Brun was here in Brighton was a joy to learn. That the lady invited her to meet her for luncheon at her rented home was a boon.

Giselle felt her spirits lift. She would enjoy renewing their friendship. More than that, she felt content that Gus and Amber were also in town to talk about her progress. She'd tell them about the failure of Jacques Durand's man to meet her the other night, and about the seeming disappearance of the guard they had hired to shadow her. Both Gus and Amber, with their husbands, and their ties to Scarlett Hawthorne's espionage network, would not only have answers for her. They would have solutions.

She strode to the window overlooking the bustling streets of the town and the wide, welcoming shoreline shimmering in the sunlight. She'd not had the pleasure of seeing Lord Carlisle since yesterday in the Lanes. She dared to hope that he would not be invited to the artist's little soirée. She doubted he would know Madame Le Brun, but then, he was a marquis, titled and therefore, to some extent or another, part of London Society. If he came, so be it. She would cope.

She inhaled, her confidence returning. She had much to do—and she would do it best if she cast off her stubborn fascination with the dashing Lord Carlisle.

"Gigi! Gigi!"

Giselle spun on the stone walk to the sound of a child calling the name her own mama had used for her. "Bella!"

The little girl broke from her father's grasp. She ran toward Giselle, her chubby arms up and waving at her.

Instinct had Giselle opening her arms wide as she bent to catch the little girl to her. "Good afternoon, dear Bella. Where are you off to?"

Carlisle towered above them. The sun silhouetting his agile form, he radiated a new joy to her day. As he always did. "Wonderful to see you, Giselle. Forgive Bella her new name for you. She has adapted it to her own abilities."

With Bella clinging to her legs, Giselle admired the elegance of him. He wore pale breeches, a peach-colored silk waistcoat, and an apple-green-and-taupe tweed frockcoat of soft wool. Her mouth watered. "I don't mind at all. Gigi is a perfectly good name. My mother used to address me that way. You have given me happy memories today. Thank you, Bella!"

The little girl giggled.

Carlisle shifted and Giselle saw his smile, brilliant as the sun. "Bella and I walk to the new carousel in the market square. A ride on a few horses is in order, you know. Where are you off to on this fine day?"

"I go to a reception. An old friend has invited me to relive our pasts."

"How lovely. Well…" He hesitated, but then took a step closer. "Why not join my sister and me for dinner?"

"Oh, I would not intrude."

"You'd be a welcome addition to our little group. Even her beau joins us." He took her hand and squeezed it affectionately. "Brighten my evening, won't you?"

Her heart swelled. "Sir, you are too complimentary."

"Allow me to be more so. Join us. Please."

"I will. I will. Thank you." She had a lump in her throat at his tender words. She surmised the gaiety of meeting old friends contributed to her sense of freedom—and abandon to accept his invitation. She tipped her head toward the walk north. "I must go."

"Eight o'clock."

"Eight it is." Unable to contain herself, she grinned at him.

"That's the look I appreciate. You, happy with me."

She blushed.

"And that look too, my dear Gigi."

"I must go."

He tsked. "*Quelle damage.*"

"You are incorrigible, sir."

"Only for you."

Reluctantly, she pulled her hand from his. "Until tonight."

CLIVE STOOD WATCHING her leave him and felt her departure as keenly as if the sun had dissolved. Eight o'clock seemed an eternity away.

She crossed the street, a graceful mirage in celestial blue.

Then he spotted a man furtively parallel her action, matching her pace.

Clive scooped up Bella into his arms and trailed behind them.

The man never diverted from his path. He was tracking her, stalking her. Thin as a stick, he was an ugly creature with the largest beak nose. Certainly he was no fine gentleman.

Who in hell was he? And what did he want with her?

Clive winced. He could not be the person she should have met outside the hotel the other night. If he were known to her or had an appointment to meet her, he would have no need to track her. He could approach her and talk.

When Giselle at last climbed the steps of a grand house and pulled the knocker, she was admitted immediately by the butler. For now, she was safe inside.

What to do to ensure that fellow did not hurt her?

Clive would hurry back to the hotel, ask Terese to take Bella to the carousel, and get Langley to help him find a man to guard Giselle. Today. *Now!*

She would be at her reception, he hoped, for at least an hour. That was all he had to ensure she was safe, unharmed. And he would do it.

After years of loneliness and self-doubt, he had found a woman he wanted for his own. He would not lose her.

Not to anyone.

She could be his.

Would be his, forever.

Chapter Nine

T HE BUTLER WHO showed Giselle up the stairs to Madame Le Brun's salon was a Frenchman with that superior attitude all French majordomos possessed. "My pleasure," he murmured to her in his Parisian accent as he opened both doors to admit her.

She nodded her thanks. One was never overly effusive with a man of his ilk. They took much as their duty, more so than their British counterparts.

But Giselle focused on her hostess. The lady sat on a long settee surrounded by two guests. Both were Giselle's friends, the very ones she had avoided meeting in the Lanes yesterday. She would have to answer for that hasty retreat, if indeed they had spotted her. So be it. She grinned at them all.

Élisabeth-Louise Vigée-Le Brun paused in her conversation and rose, hands out to greet Giselle. She was a small-boned woman with light-brown hair. She possessed an elegance to her that she long credited to her youthful exposure to those who lived at the court of Versailles. That grace she wore like a second skin, and its power drew others to her immediately.

Giselle noted that the years of the artist's exile from France had aged her with lines around her pretty eyes and silver in her soft hair. The renowned artist did Giselle the honor of embracing her.

"*Ma cherie*," the lady whispered as she kissed Giselle's cheeks. "How happy I am to see you. I am so glad you've come."

She stuck to her native language, as she had never learned any useful English, though word had it she knew a bit of Russian and German. Knowledge of German had come to her over her many years spent throughout states there. She had also lived in St. Petersburg, painting, among others, Tsar Alexander and his wife, Élisabeth, daughter of the Duke of Baden.

Amber and Gus embraced Giselle as well, then moved to facing chairs, leaving space for the newest guest and their hostess. Madame Le Brun looped her arm through Giselle's.

"Madame Le Brun," Giselle said to her mama's old friend with courtesy and the warmth of remembered happiness, "I am delighted that you found me here and invited me to your home. I had no idea you were here, else I would have announced myself to you."

"No damage," the lady went on in French, giving Giselle a hint that probably the guests at this entire party spoke that language to accommodate this famous lady. "I understand. Not an issue, I assure you. Our mutual friends, Augustine and Amber, wrote to tell me you were in residence. Now as we continue, you are Giselle and I am Élisabeth, oui? I insist." She gave a rueful shake of her head as she led Giselle to the settee. "We are old, old friends. Too old, oui?"

Madame gestured toward Amber and Gus. "Now, I know you three have known each other a long time. Correct me if my memory is poor, but did you not all attend the same Parisian finishing school?"

Giselle acknowledged Madame Le Brun's knowledge with a smile. The woman's memory for people and events had always been shockingly good. But Giselle suspected that Gus and Amber—had the topic come up before her arrival—had confirmed it already.

Giselle's affections for Gus and Amber were bountiful, the three bearing a fondness for each other born in their youth and nurtured in trials and tribulations over the years. Although their friendship had begun decades ago in a young ladies' school together, they had kept their relationship close even during the Terror. Both ladies had attended Giselle's daughter's funeral. Then in 1802, they both had come south for a visit from Paris to Blois, where Giselle continued to tend the family winery.

During that visit, Gus and Amber had secretly recruited Giselle for the work they all did together. It was then she had started to produce sketches and drawings of landscapes for them. Finally, last year, when René Vaillancourt had threatened to end her life and take her to La Force, Giselle had gotten a message to them in London about the deputy's threats. Amber and Gus had managed her escape to England with the help of Lord Ashley's former majordomo, a fellow named Corsini, and another in their network, Jacques Durand, a smuggler who worked the Channel ports as if he were more fish than man. The three women now worked together on Giselle's latest project. It kept them united and busy.

Élisabeth knew none of that and would learn none. The coincidence of their meeting here was just that. Giselle was also grateful for the cover it provided her. She could appear a woman with many friends, not a hermit keeping to her room day in and out.

"Now you must tell me of your health." Élisabeth kept Giselle's hand in hers. Other guests—ladies and gentlemen—milled about talking, laughing with each other in subdued tones. But the four women who faced each other were intent on their own conversation. "You are well?"

"Very well, merci beaucoup." Giselle wished not to speak of herself, but it was true that as a child she had been sickly. "How do you like Brighton, Élisabeth?"

"Ah, Brighton," Élisabeth sighed, content. "I am happy to bask in the sun. I do like to walk along the shore."

"How long do you remain here?" Amber was curious.

Élisabeth shrugged. "I am here only a few weeks. But then, I say that of every city I visit. The result is I overstay and bore those around me."

"We both renewed our acquaintance with Madame Le Brun in London recently," Gus said, calm and cool as ever. Her French was excellent, as she had grown up in Paris under the tutelage of her prestigious aunt, Cecily, Countess Nugent. That lady was once the friend of Josephine Bonaparte, and for many years, the infamous mistress of the old Duke of Orleans.

"We were pleased to learn you visited Brighton," Amber told Giselle in just as fine French. She had grown up with Gus as an informally adopted child of Gus's Aunt Cecily. "And so, of course, when Gus and I arrived in Brighton the other day, we sent around a note to invite madame to join us for dinner."

"I had other commitments," Élisabeth said. "But I am glad you are here today." She squeezed Giselle's hand. "Tell us, when did you arrive in England?"

"I've been here since the autumn." Giselle did not wish to be specific and reveal precisely when or how she had arrived. "I had to leave France. I could no longer bear the prejudice against those of us who had been friendly with the Bourbons." *Or those of us who object to the new dictatorship of Bonaparte and his bullies.*

"I understand," Élisabeth added with sorrow lining her pretty face. "Only a few managed to transcend the old allegiances. Lady Ashley and Lady Ramsey succeeded."

"For a while," Amber put in.

"Because of our Aunt Cecily," Gus added, "Amber and I were untouched for many years."

The ladies' aunt had been fortunate in many attachments she formed. Notably, when she was sent to Carmes prison after her lover, the duke, went to the scaffold, she lived in a cell next to a young widow, Josephine Beauharnais, now Bonaparte's wife and the Empress of France. The two women remained fast friends, and Cecily, a rich widow of a British earl before she met the French duke, benefited from the relationship.

Amber winced. "Gus's and my fortune changed with the

cancellation of the Treaty of Amiens in '03 and the fact that Gus and I married prominent Englishmen."

Gus took Amber's hand and smiled sadly. "Fouché and his second-in-command had us in their sights."

"René Vaillancourt." Élisabeth pronounced the name of the deputy director of security with disdain. "A hateful man. I despised Robespierre and his crowd of evil doers, but this Vaillancourt... Ah. I knew him when young. An assassin in the Croix Rouge Quartier. Even then, he was beautiful. Tall and suave, handsome as only evil can be. He hunts his foes mercilessly."

"We know." Amber formed the words quietly.

Élisabeth caught a breath. "He has murdered so many of my old friends..."

Giselle clutched her hands together. *Mine, too. My vintner and his wife. His four children. For the sin of opposing Bonaparte's wine taxes.* She shifted in her chair, the memory painful, sharp as a knife to her throat. Her brother had been detained by this scourge and sent to his death. So too her sister Lisette, whose only crime was a dazzling beauty and an attraction to a man unworthy of her. So she died, painfully, tragically, as he and his friend, Vaillancourt, used her so mercilessly for their pleasure.

Giselle put a hand to her forehead, her heart pounding and the memory of Lisette's punishment tearing at her and upsetting her stomach.

"Is your Aunt Cecily still in Paris?" Élisabeth asked of Amber and Gus.

Giselle set her teeth and put herself here in this friendly atmosphere. She licked her lips and recalled the question Élisabeth had asked. Yes, she had heard that her friends' aunt had helped Madame Le Brun escape Paris. Giselle believed the rumor. The countess, much like her lover, the old Orleans, had spirited many away during the Terror and afterward.

"She is," Gus said with a definite frustration. "We've urged her to leave continuously, but she refuses."

"She has lived there since she was sent by the prince regent to the old Duke of Orleans." Amber did not look pleased to say it. "She loves her house and adores her friends, including many who are in favor. She will not go. Sad to say."

Élisabeth sighed. "I was about to paint her portrait years ago, but she refused, thinking it would look poorly to spend money on art when the revolution was the topic on everyone's lips. The old duke supported the national conventions and even Robespierre. For a time. But then the tide turned, and Orleans too was arrested and sent to the guillotine."

Gus shifted in her chair, frowning and uneasy with this topic. She had known the old duke and liked him very much. "Aunt had no desire for a picture then. She was very much in love with the duke, and his loss took much life and laughter from her."

"Let us speak no more of sad things," Amber encouraged them with a soft smile.

"Exactly," agreed Élisabeth, then she turned to Giselle. "I must know, *ma petite*, if you still draw and paint."

Giselle took the question as a natural one from the lady who had taught her much about the art she pursued every day. But she would be selective about what she told her. "I do. Lately, I tend to sketch, drawing with pencil or ink. I use watercolors here in England. They give an ethereal quality to my works that I appreciate."

"Ah, oui. I understand your turn to pencil and watercolor. I have tried repeatedly to use oils here in Brighton. But the air is too humid. I cannot get the right mix to any shade I want. I have met a few old friends who live north in London. The Comte d'Artois, Louis XVI's brother, and my old friend the Comte de Vaudreuil are among those living here. Both demand of me new portraits. But I have discouraged them unless we can all go farther north, where the air is cooler—and my oils can mix!"

"I do agree," Giselle said with a nod. "Oil does work best for portraits."

"Ah, mais oui." Élisabeth looked at Giselle. "When you come

to London, I will take you to visit Vaudreuil. He thought you so talented when a child, and he will be so pleased to see how lovely you are as a mature woman."

"Merci beaucoup." Giselle had to thank her for the compliment, but she disliked Comte de Vaudreuil. He was a noted roué of obscure sexual practices. So notorious was Vaudreuil that Giselle's husband even thought him dastardly, a man to be avoided. But Vaudreuil was condemned by many for other vices. He was so friendly with Marie Antoinette that he covered her infatuation with a German count.

Influential, too, to King Louis in finance, Vaudreuil led the king into heinous debt that the Crown could not repay. Many said Vaudreuil's only good deed was that he encouraged many artists, schooled others he thought worthy, and bought their works, albeit at ridiculously low prices. He packed up many of them when he left Paris in a rush the day after the Bastille fell. He had the bad taste to brag now about their immense value. To say one good thing about him was that he was a generous benefactor to artists like Élisabeth. Some even said the two had been lovers.

"But I do not wish to intrude, Élisabeth."

"Nonsense. He loved you as child."

He loved too many as children. I managed to escape his particular interest in young girls. She would escape him now, too, and purposely not send her address to Élisabeth if and when she went to London. "He did."

"You must come," said Élisabeth. "Your skills are unique. And your talents with draftsmanship precise."

Giselle had to give the man his due for advising her as a young girl. "He was very kind to humor a child of ten who wished to draw his elaborate gardens."

From Vaudreuil, Giselle had learned the necessity of precise measurements of eye, the necessity of perspective, and the wisdom of choice of complementary color and architectural form. But she would not see him. There was his reputation to deter her. But also part of her did not wish to return to the past, not out of courtesy, nor duty. Her life in France was gone. Her skills remained, and she would use them to her benefit and Britain's. It was the only revenge she had against the likes of Vaillancourt, Fouché, and the memory of her dastardly husband.

Élisabeth was rattling on about Artois and Vaudreuil. "I also tell both gentlemen that they are much too advanced in years to wish for a portrait. An artist can do only so much to improve one's looks. Especially men who have lived hard lives." She lifted a polite finger and indicated the three ladies with her. "I would do well to paint the three of you! All ravishing women, friends who have suffered and also laughed together. Allow me to paint you!"

"Oh, Élisabeth," Gus said. "We would be honored, but we cannot take up your time when so many others are so much more important, and they are your longtime friends."

"Think nothing of it." The lady sat back. "When do you return to London?"

"A week Saturday," Amber told her. "Not enough time, I'm afraid."

Giselle knew both Amber and Gus had come to keep their appointment with her here in Brighton. Their recent note to her this morning said they should meet at the house the two ladies rented tomorrow at ten.

"When I come to London," the lady said, "I will call upon you and the three of you will name a time. Do not refuse me!"

Giselle stared into Amber's green eyes. She had no idea when she would return to London. Plus, she definitely did not want her face on any work by the famed Élisabeth Le Brun. Sought after by Vaillancourt in France, Giselle wished to remain inconspicuous here in England. Preferably along the coast while she finished her work. After that, she would like to remain inconspicuous wherever she lived.

Gus checked Amber and Giselle's faces. A flicker of defiance lived in her eyes. "Very well. We will try to find dates suitable."

Giselle hid a smile. No dates were suitable for any of the three.

Élisabeth clutched her hands together. "Superb."

"And then, Élisabeth," Gus said with a wicked smile, "you must join us for a ball. Tomorrow night in the ballroom of the Old Ship Hotel."

"Non! Non! I do not dance, *mes amis*."

Amber laughed. "Come for the conversation, then!"

Élisabeth leaned forward. "Have you invited the prince regent?"

Amber chuckled. "Oui, we have. He may not dance, but he likes to pretend he can still command the floor."

Élisabeth put a hand to her brow. "I fear the sight!"

"Don't we all!"

"Please do come," Gus told her.

"At that huge hotel on the beach?"

"Oui!"

"I will. I will." Élisabeth waggled her brows like an impulsive French lady. "For the conversation only. Now, you will forgive me, as I must see to my other guests."

When Élisabeth had gone off and was well involved with a few of her other guests, Giselle switched to English and said, "I am so happy to see you both."

"And we to see you too, Giselle," Gus said with concern in her eyes. "We saw you day before yesterday in the Lanes. Why did you not approach?"

Amber cocked her head. "Was it the presence of a certain gentleman?"

Giselle let out a breath. "Yes, it was."

"He is charming and here on holiday."

Giselle widened her eyes.

"Oh." Amber sat back. "I see. He *is* interesting."

"Alluring," teased Gus.

"You two fantasize," Giselle said with less conviction than she should.

"He is very handsome," Amber added. "A widower, you know."

"I do." Giselle tried to laugh away the subject of her enchantment with Carlisle. "Please listen to me. I need to talk with you both privately."

"Tomorrow," Gus said, a quick scan of the room allowing her a small, strained smile.

"I must tell you three things now." Giselle lowered her voice. "Our mutual friend's agent did not appear to me the other night."

"We know," Gus replied. "Do not despair. We have much to tell you in that regard. And the second problem?"

"My bodyguard has disappeared."

Amber looked stricken. "And the last problem?"

"I do believe a strange man is following me, and he resembles someone I may have seen in Hastings."

Chapter Ten

THE ASHLEYS AND Ramseys had taken a house together north
of the Steine. While in Brighton, the four usually stayed at
the Old Ship, but this week, perhaps because the weather was so
fine, the hotel was filled to capacity.

Many British—despite the threat of the Grand Army across
the Channel—had recently come to Brighton to be near the
prince regent and his entourage. Many thought it their last chance
at a brief holiday on the coast this summer. In Dover, Ramsgate,
and other towns and villages along the Channel, residents had
already packed up their belongings and headed inland. Fear of an
imminent French invasion was rampant. Army troops, such as
those stationed at Preston Barracks north of Brighton, and
volunteer home guard swamped the towns, adding to the
simmering anxiety.

Giselle hurried along the stone walkway to her friends' rented
house. They had insisted she take a hired carriage back to the
hotel yesterday—and she had allowed it. However, she had
insisted that she walk this morning. The exercise and sunshine
added a sparkle to her day. Her dashing marquis was responsible
for most of it.

Dinner last night with Carlisle, his sister Terese, and their
friend Lord Langley had been an experience she'd not enjoyed in

many years. The three of them were not only comfortable in each other's company but downright friendly. They seemed to have no conflicts with each other, merely differences of opinion. About those, they did not argue. Acceptance was the rule of the day. The two hours Giselle had spent with them reminded her of her parents' easy relationship. That was what those two had taught by example to their three children. Giselle had not known such tranquility in her own marriage. That union had been a battleground in the salon—and in bed.

The refreshing quality of dinner had been one she told Carlisle about as he stood at her door when they'd parted for the night. "I must thank you for a very pleasant evening. I have not had such a delightful experience since my parents died."

"It was but a simple dinner."

"Not to me," she'd whispered, and, on impulse, rose on her toes and kissed his cheek.

The lightning response in his silver eyes had remained as he invited her to call him by his given name. Risky as it was to accept such largesse, she had agreed with a twinkle in her eye. "My kiss invited that."

"Invite me to do more, my dear. I will not fail you."

She had believed him. He was the first man who had ever been so forward and so sweet about his regard for her. She had left him, but through the night she dreamt of walking in sylvan glades full of flowers in the sun.

Her golden memory of her dreams brought her smiling to the door of her friends.

"Good morning," the hired butler bade her, taking her gloves and pelisse. "The Ashleys and Ramseys await you upstairs. Please follow me."

Gus and Amber rushed to embrace her while their husbands politely kissed her cheek.

Lord Ashley, whom Giselle had come to know over years of friendship by his given name of Kane, had led Scarlett Hawthorne's mission to France soon after the Treaty of Amiens was signed in 1802. His responsibility there had been to enlarge the circle of espionage agents throughout the Continent while continuing to perform diplomatic and financial duties as cover for his actions. Here in Britain, he kept up his network with his wife, Gus. Their contacts here and on the Continent continued to be crucial to information about Bonaparte's regime. Giselle had benefited from those in the circle, including Corsini, Kane's former majordomo, and their contact and smuggler, Jacques Durand, who had sailed her across treacherous waters to safety in Britain.

"I am delighted to see you again, Giselle." Ashley was a tall, debonair man, dark of hair, jovial, a true diplomat by nature.

"You look well, Giselle. I am glad," said Kane's friend, Amber's husband. Godfrey DuClare, Lord Ramsey, was a different sort of fellow. Commanding in his presence, with a swarthy eminence to him, he was quick to act, quick to smile, focused always on the prize. Today, that was information.

Giselle had it for all of them.

"Will you have tea?" Gus asked her, and led her toward the assembly of settees and chairs arranged for their discussion.

"Yes, I will. Thank you." Now here with her friends, Giselle was totally relaxed. Walking north along the Steine was not a challenge to her this morning. Gus had assured her yesterday that they would assign a man to act as her guard, investigate what had happened to her other man, and search for the fellow she thought she'd seen in Hastings.

"As long as I have a new guard by tomorrow morning," she had told the two women yesterday, "I would prefer to walk to meet you. All of that exposure adds to my ability to draw the city accurately...and inaccurately."

Her argument that she doubted anyone would hurt her in broad daylight had been met with skepticism. The use of a carriage back to the hotel was the result. But today, coming here, she had felt the presence of others interested in her. She wondered if they all spied upon each other and inspired an unusual parade!

Now, Gus and Amber sat on the settee to either side of Giselle. The two men stood, Ashley motionless behind one facing chair, Ramsey breaking his stillness now and then to prowl the room.

"We have no word yet on what has happened to your first guard," Ashley told her.

"We have two men investigating that," Ramsey added. "We hope for news later today."

"How is the new man?" Gus asked.

"Attentive," Giselle said. "I walked the beach early this morning and felt his presence. Benevolent. I am pleased."

"Does the fellow who resembles one from Hastings follow you today?"

"I think so."

"Shall we hire an additional guard?" Amber asked.

"No. One is enough." *Provided nothing happens to him.* "You will tell me what happened to my first man, I do hope."

Ramsey frowned. "I won't have you frightened, Giselle."

She was not his wife and not a child. "I want to know."

Ramsey acceded to that. "As you wish."

"And what happened to Jacques Durand's messenger that he did not appear the other night? Do you know?"

Ashley winced. "He was arrested hours before he was to meet you."

"Bow Street Runners took him?"

"No," Ashley said. "Revenuers who tracked him from Durand's schooner offshore."

Giselle took her tea from Gus's hands and sipped. That news was not good. She liked Durand, his crew, and his canny ability to outwit the French and British blockade. She had sailed with him last September from Le Havre to Dover. He had been good company on their many days at sea. They'd even discussed the construction of the French fleet in La Rochelle and Le Havre, both ports Giselle had investigated before she met Durand in an inn in Le Havre. He was a skilled sailor, and Giselle would not see him harmed or hurt. Now she was worried not only about Durand but also their friend and agent in the encampment of the Grand Army in Boulogne. Bonaparte assembled most of the flat-bottomed boats of his invasion fleet there in sight of his army generals to encourage them for the future crossing.

"Durand is vital to us. He will look for his man and rescue him, I hope."

"Of course," Amber assured her with a touch of her hand.

Giselle knew that meant if and when Durand could get in and out of whatever Channel port he currently hid inside.

"We need all our links unbroken," said Ashley.

"And the information flowing. However," Ramsey said with a frown, "we have to tell you of our other challenges."

Giselle put down her cup and saucer on the small tea table.

"Your last drawings that we had you place in the book in that store in Hastings remain there."

"No one has picked them up?" She tipped her head, surprised. All her other postings had been carried off as planned by those they suspected as French agents. They had proof of that from other agents, and the actions of the French confirmed their belief in Giselle's false drawings. "Why do you suppose that is?"

"We have no idea," Ashley admitted. "We can only wait to see if someone comes to take them away."

Giselle grew uneasy and put a hand to her brow. "Do you still believe the one who will buy the book is a double agent?"

Ramsey nodded. "We do. We have planted the lie among those we think are double agents that good drawings of the town are in that book. We have a list of those whom we suspect send information of our troop numbers and movements to Boulogne."

"That list comes from Lord Appleby's wife Vivienne?" Giselle had never met the lady but had heard her life story from Gus and Amber after she had arrived in London months ago. All four of them here had met the woman who had imitated her older sister in order to return to France and learn the fate of their middle sister. What Vivienne had learned from René Vaillancourt's lips was that her sister was not only a French spy herself, but she ran a network of them here in Britain.

"It does," Ramsey said. "Viv has been very helpful in that. Her older sister sent her a list of names before she died."

Vivienne's older sister, Charmaine Massey, had been a famous Drury Lane actress. As Charmaine made her way into the bedrooms of British politicians, she had also sent to Vaillancourt all the news she collected.

Vivienne had discovered her sister's treachery from Vaillancourt himself. When she arrived in England with her new husband, Tate Cantrell, the Earl of Appleby, Viv had confronted Charmaine with her betrayal. Charmaine had planned nothing less than setting up Viv to take the blame for all her double dealing. When Viv vowed never to see her sister again, Charmaine—who was dying—hoped to resurrect any fondness from her youngest sister. So she revealed the names of her friends and double agents to Viv. It was that valuable list of names that aided Scarlett Hawthorne's network here in Britain to capture Bonaparte's spies.

Giselle glanced at Amber and Gus. "I had hoped to be finished with my drawings of Brighton before now. Because I was unsure about my guard, I confess that I have not done as much research as I usually do. To complete them, I need a few more days."

"You have it," Amber assured her.

"Go out about town now with the added security of our new man," Ramsey said.

"I will." Giselle picked up her tea once more. "But I worry. Summer is the best season for Bonaparte to sail toward us. I wonder if our time grows short to make an impression on the shipbuilders for the dimensions of those flat-bottom boats."

Ashley came round to sit in a chair and lean toward Giselle. "We've learned from our agent in Boulogne that the French draftsmen of their navy have changed the shore elevations for their amphibious landing craft."

"How have they changed them? When?" she asked, frightened all her work was for naught. Everyone on this project knew that the French designers of naval ships were not qualified shipwrights. Their practices were never uniform, and one ship might be seaworthy, another not. Many were so poorly designed that they were potentially deadly to the crew. Many a ship's crew had to pump water from the hull to keep it from sinking. Many fell apart after one voyage.

The worrisome news more than a year ago, that the French shipbuilders questioned the depth of English shore elevation, had been the impetus for Giselle's drawings. That and her own desire to foil the French and gain freedom for herself in a land other than the one of her birth had become her goals.

Ashley folded his hands. "We've learned that their amphibious landing ships have flaps that drop into rock and sand."

"How deeply?" Giselle envisioned the challenges of the French. "They must want their soldiers to wade ashore easily from those boats."

"Exactly," said Ashley.

"Fully armed, too," added Ramsey.

"So…how deeply do those flaps drop into rock and sand?" She held her breath.

"Sadly, we do not know the dimensions of the new flaps," Ashley said. "Our agent there tells us she knows only that they've changed them as per new intelligence."

She? A woman was their agent in Boulogne? Giselle knew they had an agent in the encampment in Boulogne. But she had never imagined that person might be a woman.

"And that whatever the dimensions of the flaps," Ramsey added, "all are the same."

Giselle did not know whether to laugh or cry at her next conclusion. "So they will use the same amphibious ships for all coastal cities?"

"You drew Dover, Margate, and Eastbourne with approximately the same elevations. Those are likely invasion points. Do draw Brighton with a different sea elevation," Ramsey urged her.

"Higher or lower, it matters not. The French must think the elevations of the least likely ports of call are of a different dimension. In variety there is believable viability."

"We can pray," said Ashley, "that their landing flaps are for deeper water than necessary."

"So that when their soldiers do try to wade ashore from those boats," she said with satisfaction, "they drown."

The horror of thousands of soldiers in their armor and with weapons drawn floating dead in the English Channel paralyzed her. However, only for a moment. Defeat of Bonaparte's plan was a victory. Success was a magical freedom.

Might she soon be finished with her work? Then she could concentrate on other things, cooking and flowers and perhaps even a bit of fun. Might she go so far as to allow herself the enchantment of having an affair?

"We need to finish the job," Ashley said.

"So our line of sketches look complete," she added. "And they have no fear they have been duped."

"Until they realize it occurred at the hand of their own misinformed French agent." Ashley grinned.

Ramsey showed his own pleasure with a wry half-smile. "Meanwhile, our agent in Boulogne says Boney harasses his admirals to stop whining about the winds and tides—and make a plan to invade."

Amber frowned. "We need to get them off the coast. People here are beside themselves with worry. Their shouts as they drill scare everyone."

Ramsey looked at his wife with misery in his dark gaze. "They have benefited from their stay."

Ashley winced. "Two years now."

Ramsey stared at his friend. "Boney has organized each corps into its own small army. They have in their corps structure not just infantry, cavalry, and artillery, but intelligence, medical, engineering, and transport."

Amber sniffed. "Their army is better than their navy. They

could build fast ships better than we, but now if they attempt to land here, they will strike with this defective flotilla. Better to stay home in Normandy, don't you think?"

"Parade around and yell at us from the coast, yes!" said Ashley.

"Still," Giselle said, her mind on her own responsibility, "this works best if the drawings in the Hastings book shop are picked up. Brighton, too."

Ramsey shook his head. "Nothing we can do about Hastings or here. We can only expect that their agent will show up in both places because Bonaparte demands his armada sail, and sail soon."

Amber took Giselle's hand. "Don't you worry about that."

"I want this to work, Amber. I want them all defeated."

"With what you have done, Giselle," Ashley assured her, "we will succeed."

Chapter Eleven

GISELLE HIRED A maid to help her dress for the Ashleys' and Ramseys' ball. Servants were not people she had dealt with regularly in years. In many ways, she preferred living simply and on her own. But formal attire required attention to the front, the back, the darn corset and strings, and the drape of the décolleté and the hem. *Mon Dieu.* What a fuss! But the new royal-purple silk from the modiste in the Lanes was a glorious choice of fabric, color, and—she could say—drama, too.

"Just this, madam." The young maid was good, belying her few years at her work. "Your corsage is…um…"

"The modiste," Giselle replied to the maid eyeing the daring cut of the bodice a fraction of an inch above the line of her nipples, "wishes me to catch a man."

The girl blinked at her with dark eyes filled with concern.

"I make a joke, Mary. I asked the woman to improve the line of the bodice, but she took me to mean lower it." Giselle sighed, smiling at the girl in their reflection in the mirror. "We have both done our best."

"The purple is like heaven, madam." The maid stepped back to admire the full ensemble. "I understand there are many gentlemen invited tonight. Dukes and such. Maybe even the regent. You will attract them all."

If Carlisle—Clive—were in attendance, Giselle would want only him. Tonight, she felt safe, protected. She was not going out, only down the main stairs to the ballroom. She could enjoy the wine, the music, and a bit of freedom from worry.

"You are kind, Mary." She picked up her fan of delicate ivory sticks and slid the ribbon of it on her wrist. "I know my hostesses and their husbands, so I will be in good company."

The maid virtually danced toward the door, while her eyes widened in humor. "I will tidy your rooms, madam. Please do ring for me to help you undress. I will be happy to help you."

"I will, Mary. Merci beaucoup." Giselle stepped through the door into the hall.

As the girl closed the door behind her, Giselle told her blood to stop singing in her ears. This was to be a prestigious ball, so had said the *Brighton Gazette* this morning. It was a formal event where only the best people—the titled, the rich and famous— came to socialize. She had nothing to fear from any of them. If her beak-nosed shadow were among them, she had poorly misjudged his class, income, and purpose. But then, she had not seen him today, and she could conclude he had returned to his lair. Perhaps he was deterred by the appearance of her new bodyguard, or simply dropped his interest in her. Which was a good thing, since she itched to be done with her drawings of Brighton. She'd worked on what estimates she had collected and remained indoors working. She'd not even gone up to the Downs to view Brighton's topography from that advantage.

She flicked open her fan like a coquette. Tonight, she would have fun.

THE MUSIC OF the orchestra floated out to her as she rounded the grand staircase and headed for the Old Ship's ballroom. The Ashleys and the Ramseys stood at the entrance greeting guests.

Most ladies came with an escort. Giselle had none, but then, she was comfortable with her lack of protocol, given she was with old, dear friends.

"Ah, here is our Giselle." Kane, the Earl of Ashley, heralded her arrival as Gus kissed both her cheeks. "I am thrilled to see you again, mon cherie."

"As am I to see you looking so well," she told him. They would make it sound as if the five of them were not yet friends. The walls could have ears. She had learned that so well in Blois, when Vaillancourt had put his people into her household staff to report on her to him. "I think our Augustine has smoothed your brows. You appear to have fewer worries."

"Flattery gets you in the door, Giselle," Amber welcomed her.

"I have more silver hair, Giselle!" Lord Ramsey was a dark, beautiful man fit for a lady's most erotic dreams.

Giselle laughed with all four of them. But to Amber she lifted a brow. "You really must do something to make Godfrey more at ease."

"I have tried," Amber said as she rolled her green eyes. "The man is ever vigilant. I have no time to read or draw. He is constantly taking me riding or walking."

"She feeds me too well, Giselle," Ramsey added. "I must fence and box to stay fit."

"What he does," his wife joked, "is play with the children so often that they don't recognize their nannies."

He swept an arm around his wife's waist. "They know you, my darling. That's all they'll ever need."

"Which is why"—Amber bent as if to share a secret—"we will soon welcome a third child to our family."

"Oh, that is wonderful! Congratulations!" Giselle said. They had a boy and girl. To have another child was a blessing.

And I am envious.

She cleared her throat. "I wonder if Madame LeBrun has arrived."

"She has." Gus pointed toward the far corner. "She asked for you."

"I will go to her."

Ashley and Ramsey gave her small bows.

Ashley said, "We will dance, Giselle."

"As ever before," Ramsey added.

"I look forward to it, but your toes do not!" she said, and with that, she tipped her head toward the corner where she could find her friend, Élisabeth.

Giselle sailed over and greeted the lady with a smile. Standing talking with her was Terese, Lady Winterton, Clive's pretty sister. "Good evening, Giselle. Delightful to see you again."

Her words were honest. Giselle and Terese had enjoyed each other's company each time they met. Dinner the other evening included.

"A large crowd, isn't it?" *Is Clive here?*

"Quite a crush," Terese agreed. "I've not seen such a gathering in years. But then, I do not attend balls as a regular rule."

"I prefer afternoon events myself," Giselle admitted. "Garden parties are more my favorite."

"And you, Madame Le Brun?" Terese asked Élisabeth.

"The afternoon is for conversation and the evening is for family and laughter."

"I do agree," came the resilient baritone of a tall, warm presence beside Giselle. Clive held three glasses of pale white wine, which he handed round to the women.

"Oh, take mine, please, monsieur le marquis," begged Élisabeth. "Do not fetch another. I came to the party to be personable. I remain for only a few minutes."

Terese shook her head. "Absolutely, you must remain. The prince regent has accepted the invitation. Everyone is abuzz."

Beside her, Giselle felt the solidity of Clive, whose shoulder touched hers in an intimacy that rocked her. She looked up into his perfect gray eyes and traced his lips with her gaze. She took a sip of her wine and licked her lower lip. How she wanted the taste of him on her tongue. The feel of him beneath her fingertips. The intensity of his fascination with her proven, inside her. She had not wanted any man as she did this charming one.

Oh, she was besotted!

She tore her attentions to more proper thoughts. "Stay, Élisabeth. Everyone must see the prince at his leisure."

The lady smothered a laugh. "I am used to the vanities of the powerful. He thinks himself handsome, I suppose."

"Always," Clive confirmed.

"Come, madame," Terese said to Élisabeth, "I'd like to introduce you to a mutual friend of ours."

The two ladies drifted away toward Lord Langley, who had eyes only for Terese.

"They have gone so that we can talk," Clive said, his large presence hovering over Giselle, his hand to hers. "I missed seeing you on the beach this morning. I went out alone. Bella had a nightmare and a cough."

"Oh! Is she well?"

"Better. The spring air, we have learned, aggravates her throat. But she recovers."

"And you?" she asked, dissolving into a haze of desire with the way he looked at her. "You are well?"

"I am now, to see you. I was up for hours and slept late. Did you not go walking this morning?"

"I went as dawn broke."

"Is that as refreshing as later, when the sun kisses the surf and sand and rocks?"

She rolled a shoulder, smiling. "You know my preference."

"Of course I do. I saw you that first day we met. To look at you was to understand all you enjoy."

His words were as mellow as his expression—and she watched how his full mouth formed words. The man had lips a woman would savor. Firm and plush, wide with a smile now.

"What is it?" he asked her, nigh unto a whisper. "You conquer me with a look."

She dragged her eyes up over his flesh, his straight aquiline nose, the wide arch of his brows, the almond shape of his gray, long-lashed eyes. "You are the devastating one, sir. Perfection for a portrait."

Somehow, someway, he took her elbow, his fingers gliding to her waist. He was all light and humor—and her every breath yearned for his nearness. "I'd give the earth for one of you."

Complimented, she wished to be the only woman he ever wanted. "A high price for a painting that I could never let you pay."

He stepped so near, she inhaled his bergamot cologne and his abject devotion to his promise. "I would. Let me."

His whispered words swept through her like an elixir. Her mind was filled with a golden vision of what it would be like to be loved by this man. Deft yet ravishing, he would consume her…and she would let him.

Let him. Match him. Enjoy him.

She cast around for sanity and something to proclaim to him. "I have not known such praise…or such an invitation to rapture."

He toyed with a frown, beneath which stood a scorching-hot smile. "With me, you would know it all."

He meant capable of love.

Torn between having him and rejecting all he offered, she fought with herself to deter him. "I tried years ago to do a self-portrait. It was a disaster. I honor others by never attempting their portrait, either. One must know one's limitations and stick to one's skills."

"What are your skills, then?" He was all curiosity and light, accepting her turn of conversation to a topic less intoxicating. "Tell me who and what you are."

"Ah. Well." He was not to be waylaid in his pursuit. But she would see him held in abeyance and stuck to practicalities. "When I have time? Cooking. Roses and tulips. Landscapes."

"Ah." A flicker of darkness flashed over his features. "Pastorals, or what? Seascapes?"

"Oui, both."

"I should like to see them."

"They are not worthy of examination, sir."

"It's time you left off with 'sir' and 'my lord.' I am Clive to you. As you are dear to me."

She opened her mouth to object.

A wicked smile curled the edges of his fabulous lips. "If you say it is too soon, I will take that as promise that there will be a future."

She went wistful, the impossible not hers to claim. But she would reveal what she could…and hope not to delude him. "Oh, Clive, I surrender. I could hope there is a future, but—"

"There is." He crushed her close. She cared not that others would see or object. To be held by him, seduced with words by him, set her aloft with a thrill she'd never known. "I would make it so."

"If time permitted—"

"It does, my dear. I command it to be." He smiled, forcing all her anxiety to drift away. "If you do not come with me to the floor, my Gigi, I will kiss you here now and in such passion that—"

She caught her breath. Two fingers to his lips, she perceived how others paused to stare.

"No kissing?" He arched a devilish, long blond brow. "Then we must dance."

"Clive…please."

"I will please you and myself, and soon. Now, come. We are dancing." He took her glass and put it away, then led her out onto to the chalked floor. "This that the master has called a country dance. Simple and a bit of fun. I'd say, sweetheart, you need some fun."

Sweetheart. No one had called her that for so many years. Her papa had. Never her husband. What was Clive doing to her to tear down her past and create the shining lure of a love affair with him? "Fun. So rare a treat. I think, Clive, you are too prescient."

"Thank goodness for that, then." He held out his hand, and

even through the fabric of her silk gloves she could feel his hunger for her.

She glanced about as they took up a place in the square drawn upon the floor. "You must tell me what to do. I've danced in Blois and Paris, but not here."

"You will do beautifully. Just follow my lead."

The formations were simple, just as Clive described them. The dance was easy as a breeze, and Giselle found herself smiling at him as they parted, faced other partners, then reunited, only to walk hand in hand down a long line of dancers and return to their four-squared positions.

"That was more fun than I anticipated." She would give him that. After all, she'd been so standoffish that she might have, at any point, alienated him. And she had no desire to do that. Not any longer. She wanted him…closer.

"Would you care for another glass of wine now?"

"I would."

He spun around. "Ah, a footman. We needn't hunt at all."

She took the flute from his long fingers and allowed the frisson of his touch to do its work. This man seemed to flow in her blood, whisper to her heart and linger there.

"Shall we stroll on the balcony? The night is soft," he said with a look of innocence on his face.

"Let's." She asked for trouble. Friendship with him—with anyone—was not recommended. Not until she finished her final project. But she'd been captured by his determination to be her swain. She should not allow her appreciation for his face and form to influence her need to fill her lonely days, let alone her bleak, cold nights. But he persisted, and she was conquered. Now she wanted him. Tonight.

Few took the air on the balcony, so the two of them wandered to one side. The abutting wall blocked the wind that whirled up from the sea and created a calm nook in which to stand and drink and talk.

"How long do you remain in Brighton?" he asked her, nonchalant, as if he had not mesmerized her with sensuous longing inside the ballroom.

"Indefinitely." Though that was the truth, she could not predict her departure.

"Do you plan to stay in the hotel?"

"Perhaps." Did he want to offer an interlude with him? Her heart jumped at the hope. "It affords me privacy, and I prefer that."

He knitted his brows, and in the silhouette he presented to her, she saw a man confounded. "You have that special grant from His Majesty's Government that permits you to visit on the southern shore."

The visa that he'd mentioned before was a paper she guarded with her life. "I do. I can stay as long as I wish."

He frowned, his concern dark. "To have received it, you must have friends in high places."

"Friends of friends." She would tell him nothing more. She did not have to. He could see evidence of that tonight with this invitation from the Ashleys and Ramseys. From that, he might wonder if she also knew Scarlett Hawthorne and her chief clerk, Todd Carlton. But she would not tell him.

He gave her a searing sidelong glance...and changed the subject. "Bella asks for you. Won't you meet us tomorrow morning for a walk and a kite fly?"

Oh, how she wanted to do that. Fly and laugh. Find freedom again. "You test me and tempt me."

"I won't stop."

"You should."

"You should accept my invitation. Bella would be so happy." He was once more a man, enraptured, whispering, "And so would I."

"I find it difficult to...to..." she said, gulping past her desires and her griefs. "Oh, Clive, I look at Bella and I see my daughter."

"And?"

"She is gone. Dead these past three years. But I see Bella and my heart lifts. It's a new and startling feeling for me."

"A way to heal, I think." He drew near and enveloped her with a tenderness that made her heart yearn and her knees weak.

She faced the dark night and the rolling sea. By the light of the moon, she could see the rounding arch of white surf as it rushed to the shore. "I have carried my grief over her loss with me for so long that I am surprised to find it waning when I laugh with Bella."

His arms went around her, and as if she had not proof enough before now of how much taller and sturdier he was, she leaned into him and found safe harbor.

He kissed the crown of her hair. "To have lost her must have been a trial."

"She was my laughter and my sunshine. After she was gone, I could find none for ever so long."

He stroked the hair at her nape. "And now?"

"The other day, I saw a moment's hell when Bella ran into the sea. It was like losing my girl all over again. I could not—" She burrowed against him, tears burning her eyes. "I could not let her go."

"Thank God you did not." He lifted her chin. "Cry. It helps. I am here to catch your tears." He touched her cheek, his fingertips an angel's touch as he caught a teardrop.

How could she want this man so dearly? He was a stranger, a beautiful fortress of a man, but she had needed him—hadn't she?—for all her life.

⋙⋘

HE BRUSHED HER bottom lip with the pad of his thumb. She was soft and yielding, her eyes closing, her long lashes sweeping the arch of her cheeks. He had never wanted to comfort and keep a woman so desperately. So completely.

"I want to kiss you," he whispered, tormented by the

knowledge that he should wait. He should think. He should treat her with all the patience a worthy lover would grant her.

Her answer had her opening her eyes, caressing him with them—and making him yearn for her.

He gathered her up. She was so delicate, fragile as china, yet firm and resilient, all eager woman. He pressed her torso to his. Her breasts were lush and hard.

He took her mouth, a gentle claim at first that quickly turned to triumph and the wild desire for more.

She mewled, lifted her arms around his neck, and ran her fingernails up through his hair. She wanted him.

He swelled with pride and broke away, breathless.

"Again," she murmured, and rose on her toes to frame his face with cool, soft hands.

He'd not deny her nor himself. He groaned and lifted her off her feet and whirled her to the wall, to the alcove where, in his maddening need for her, he hoped they had some seclusion.

Yet when her lips were on his once again, he confirmed only that this luscious woman wanted him. He took her mouth, a brazen claim. He could not stop.

Only for breath did he tear his lips from hers.

"Come upstairs."

His burning brain barely fathomed her words.

She drew his face down to hers with a hand to his nape and kissed him with an urgency he'd rarely known from a woman.

"Come. Won't you?"

He'd be a fool to deny her or himself. But he had to be wise, go slowly—not devour her but treasure her. "Leave me first," he told her, his mouth to her ear. "I will follow in a few minutes."

"Come now."

"I can't, sweetheart." He grasped her hand and put it to his lower belly. He dare not move it lower, but her blue eyes flickered in knowledge and delight. He smiled, but the pain of parting from her was like cold water to his veins. "Go."

She drew away, unsure, yet eager. "You'll hurry?"

He put a finger to her mouth and drew her soft, plush lower lip down. "I am there now. Go!"

She picked up her skirts and disappeared into the ballroom in a wild rustle of royal-purple silk.

He ran a hand through his hair. Was he foolish? Did he care? *Yes! For her!*

And logic—that element which had ruled his life since his marriage failed—flew to the stars.

He bit his lip. He must not regret this night. He'd go upstairs. He had promised. He'd walk inside her rooms, and yes, by God, he would kiss her again.

But that would be all. That would be enough for tonight.

Chapter Twelve

S HE FLEW INTO her rooms, flinging wide the door, anticipation thumping in her heart. She wanted this man. It was silly, girlish, daring to want a man she barely knew. But he was kind and honorable. She knew that in her bones.

And he is infatuated with me.

She stood, stock still, her gaze on the square patch of hall carpet, and willed him to appear. She closed her eyes and, in her enchantment, saw him before her. Tall and sturdy, a bulwark against the winds and misfortunes of life, a magnificent man who appealed to every one of her senses. Silver and gold, indelibly etched on her mind as a jewel of a man.

Yes, she wanted him. He was gentleman enough to care for her reputation. He was enchanted enough to accept her invitation.

And if he doesn't come?

Sorrow pierced her like an arrow to her chest. Well, then, if he did not come, he was kind enough to ignore her impulsiveness and save her face. They could be friends, if not lovers.

Certainly, there was that.

But in a second, there he was, standing at her door, not crossing unless she would still take him.

Joy flashed through her as she strode forward, her fists

clenched on his formal black frockcoat, to lead him inside.

He walked toward her, his handsome face that of a boy who asks for nothing in this world but kindness. "If you have changed your mind—"

"Non." She pulled him toward her.

He came…like a sleepwalker, but shut the door behind him with a foot to the wood. In the next moment, she was in his arms once more. He had her up against him, her height no issue, as he had her up off her feet.

His lips on hers, she clasped him tightly to her, his shoulders, his strength, the silk of his hair through her fingers all she cared to have.

He carried her to the settee near the fireplace and sat her in his lap. She melted into him, kissing his jaw, undoing his cravat.

He cupped her cheek. "Look at me."

She shook her head. He'd tell her to stop. Give her some reason to deny what they should be doing here.

"Sweetheart, we—"

She gulped back her sorrow that he'd leave. "You know how to kiss."

"What?" He laughed.

She brushed her lips on his. "You are so good at kissing."

He lifted her chin. "Darling, this art takes two. And you know how to kiss."

"Do I?" That shocked her.

His eyes were faceted in shades of curiosity and desire. "You know how to thrill me with your lips."

She sank closer to him. "I am so very glad."

"And you deserve to be kissed."

"Well," she said with a wide-eyed glance.

"And often," he added.

"By you." She nuzzled his cheek.

"Only by me."

"Oh, yes. No other. Let me," she begged him, "let me have more of you."

He pulled away, the arch of his brows and the caution in his eyes showing her his thought that she meant more. "I... No, we shouldn't."

She dropped little kisses to the firm curve of his lips. With one hand, she learned the contours of his biceps and his corded torso. She'd had her husband...or rather, he had had her. Often and in moods more of dominance and possession rather than the tenderness or love. She'd had other lovers, briefly, as a means to slake desire. With none had she found more than physical fulfillment. With this man, she knew she would have more, give more, find more than she had with any man. "Oh, Clive, we should."

He sucked in a breath and shook his head. "Giselle. Soft and sweet. It suits you. All of you."

"And you are Clive. Darling, daring Clive who knows how to kiss a lady."

"Ah, Giselle, my lovely. I know how to kiss you."

"Then do not stop." She put her lips to his. "Never stop."

He held her away from him, his gray eyes full of reluctance. The gentleman again came forth, and she loved him for it. "You are certain?"

"Never more so."

He put her to the settee, got to his feet, and turned to scoop her into his arms, then marched through to her bedroom. He stood her by the bed and turned her away from him. In the hushed silence of the night, the music from the ballroom drifting up and curling around her euphoria, he worked on her gown and put it to a chair. Then her stays, but he left her in her chemise.

Then he spun her toward him.

She held the muslin up with one hand to her chest. "Don't think."

"No." He plucked pins from her coiffure. "There is no logic here. Not tonight. My God," he crooned as he threaded his fingers through the wealth of her hair and spread it over her bare shoulders. "You are a beautiful dream. Giselle." He murmured her name as he drew her near him and took her lips in a savage kiss. "Giselle."

As he broke away, she lifted her arms and let fall the cotton shift.

He gasped.

She smiled to herself. She was not shy, had not been since her husband had made her parade her bare skin before him. But this, with this man, was so different. He gazed upon her nakedness not as prurient display, but in his soft gray desire stood a reverence that took her breath away.

He unbuttoned his frockcoat and waistcoat and shrugged out of them, allowing them to grace the floor, no time, no need to pick them up.

His shirt came over his head. Suddenly it was her turn to gasp. Her turn to admire. Her turn to kiss the wealth before her. His clavicle. His breastbone. His nipple. The crisp hair that began on his chest and wended down beneath his breeches.

His hands were atop hers, unbuttoning, pushing away what separated them. He toed off his shoes and sat her on the bed. Naked save for his socks, he removed her slippers. With care, he undid her garters and slid down her stockings.

In a moment, he opened wide her legs and looked at the junction of her thighs. His fingers he wrapped around her ankles, slid them up her calves to part her aching folds and lace his fingers in her nether hair. "Giselle. You are so lovely."

She arched, giving him wider access. Her pulse racing, her body wet and needy.

He was so reverent, tears rose to her eyes. But this was no occasion for sadness. It was a time for earthy smiles and sighs.

She sank back on the bed, one elbow to the mattress, one hand leading him to cover her.

He was hot, heavy and so gentle, a kiss made of sunlight and midnight desire, a caress of wind and fire. She had never imagined a man could be so indescribably sweet in bed.

He dragged her up beneath him and spread her out, her arms

wide, his long legs between her own. He dipped his head to inhale the lavender scent she'd put in her hair. Then he kissed her shoulder, the hollow of her throat, and the center between her breasts. He laved her nipple, sucking her to a point and letting her go to admire his handiwork. Grinning, he put his lips around it again and sucked her up so slowly, so powerfully, that she groaned at his ardor.

Between her thighs, she felt his hardened cock. He nestled himself against her hungry lips and probed for the center of her. He was all flame and power as he took himself in hand and painted her wet folds with his tip as if he rendered her his art, he the master artist, she his canvas.

Yearning to blossom in the color and form he saw, she bucked up. "More," she told him, as she had on the balcony. "Much more."

Her eyes closed in the ecstasy he produced, she thrashed her head as he separated her flesh and stroked her to wild readiness. "Please," she urged him when she could take no more without him.

And he, good man, obliged her. He took himself in hand and, with excruciating slowness, sank bit by bit into the fullness of her.

"Ohh," was all she could say as she lay quite still, not daring to move for the brilliance that blinded her.

"I know," he gritted out, nipping her ear. "You are delicious, my darling."

She grinned at him. "Not half as wonderful as you, my dear man."

"Let's test that, shall we?"

She dug her nails into the smooth, taut skin of his back. "Start now. I need you."

The essence of his loving was a blur of thrust and parry, a bliss of ravishing sweetness that rocked her. He took her mouth as he took her body in bold, long strokes, endlessly, in mindless madness. And when he touched a certain part of her with his fingers, she exploded with delight. Her pulsing result sang through her, and his loud, long groan of climax was her finest reward.

She lay there, panting, as he rolled to his side.

He turned her to him and brushed the tendrils of hair from her lips. "You are spectacular, my darling."

"I did so little."

He cupped her cheek and had her look at him. "You wanted me, and I you." He took her lips in a sultry kiss. "That is the charm."

"I've never had that."

He used his thumb to outline her lips. "Your husband did not take care with you."

"Not like you." She stared at him and told the truth. "Not like this. I have never felt so…"

"Wanted."

"Filled. Complete."

His eyes blazed with triumph. "Neither have I."

"Your wife did not like…?"

"The marriage bed?" He shook his head. "No."

"Were you good together? Otherwise?"

He ran his hand down her arm to her waist to rest on her belly. "She didn't like disarray. The muddle. The mess, she called it. She feared for pregnancy and complained. She would come to me and offer herself up like a sacrifice, claiming her duty was to give me an heir. We…learned to go about this mating thing as an event. She did get pregnant just once. The result is the delightful Bella."

He was so distressed, his brows knitted together, his magnificent mouth strained, and she could not see him so sorrowful. She put her hand atop his and led him to cup her. There, she led his fingers inside her. "I love you inside me. Have me again."

He dropped a quick kiss to the tip of her breast. "I would not want to make you hate me."

"You could never."

"Or make you sore and uncomfortable."

"Well," she said with a wide-eyed laugh, "you must make love to me again to learn if that is true."

"An invitation I cannot refuse," he said against her lips as he opened her to his hardened cock. "You are my ecstasy."

"And you are mine."

HE ROSE UP on one arm and stared at the naked beauty beside him. He'd slept, exhausted. They'd had each other three times, and he could not recall if he'd been responsible that first time and left her before he had his climax. The irresponsibility of that tore at his good spirits. He would not shame her.

He remembered she had come fully to her own completion each time they had loved. Pride blossomed in his heart at that. She was as irresistible now that they'd united as when he first saw her, truly saw her, on the beach.

He smiled to himself. Was that only days ago?

She sighed in her sleep and snuggled against him. Her midnight hair curled around him like silken threads. Her complexion was pure, her cheeks—dare he say?—darker, rosier since they'd found delight together.

He wrapped his arm around her waist and pressed himself along the elegant lines of her body. Her throat, her pointed breasts—her large, luscious nipples, soft belly, and shapely legs were perfection.

How had he won this lady to her bed?

From the intrigue of spying her on the shore to her rescue of Bella, he could not seem to see enough of her. She filled his sight with her uniqueness, her frankness. Her odd venture that first night when she waited for someone who did not appear mystified him. With that, he sought to find in her the reasons for such an event. Yet his view of her colored more brightly each time they met. His perspective of her nature widened as he saw she had facets to her nature that raised more questions. Who was she that she took such risks?

Then in the ballroom, he'd seen her in that gown of ethereal purple and nearly lost his footing. His head had spun. She was beautiful to him before the ball, but in that crowded hall, she was an angelic vision—and he had to have her.

Have her in his arms. To dance, yes. But more, more. And he had forgotten how to properly court a lady.

A widower of two years now, he was a respected single man. Many young ladies and their eager mothers had set their sights on him. Still he had not found any who interested him. But he was a man who had viewed a woman whom he desired only once before. A man who had rushed to judgment and asked her to marry him. A man who'd regretted the proposal and spent years lost to his wife's indifference to his infatuation, his seduction, and any charms he assumed he naturally possessed.

Loath as he was to leave Giselle, he should. Hotel staff would be up and circulating the halls before dawn. He would not wish to have gossip spread among them of his night here with her.

"You think of leaving," she whispered in husky, sleep-filled distress.

He pulled this darling lady against him. Craving her luscious body and priding himself on her desire for him, he dropped a kiss to the crown of her hair.

She stretched her long legs, then looped one over his. Her head turned up toward his, and her dreamy eyes held longing.

"I did not mean to wake you," he whispered.

But she kissed him. "I felt you watching me."

"Wanting you," he corrected her, and took her lips again. "I must go."

Sorrow turned down the corners of her mouth.

His conceit that she could crave him grew a thousand-fold.

She turned petulant and rubbed her breasts against his chest. "The music has ended. They've all gone to bed. What time do you think it is?"

"I'll get my watch in my frockcoat." He began to push away.

"Don't look." She drew him back, curling her fingers around his nape. "I don't care what time it is. Stay. Stay, won't you?"

"Sweetheart, you know that is not wise. Servants may soon be in the halls. Guests, too."

She pressed her lips to his throat, her thighs opening, her hands pressing him near. She was all wild, willing woman, and she was his.

He could not resist her squirming invitation. He was hard again.

"You want me," she announced with a little giggle and a firm press of her center to his cock.

"I dare not. I fear if we do this again, I may never leave."

She slid her hand down to cover him. Her caress was firm, rhythmic.

She had him shaking his head. "We must be prudent."

She fell back to the bed, her eyes squeezed shut. "You're right. And you'll think me a wanton." She took his words as rejection for all they had done.

He could not allow that. "I think you daring and lovely and wise to want me."

She smiled at him, her torment gone. "Wise, eh?"

"I am a good catch. I have everything you could need." Was he a fool to offer himself so baldly? He did not care.

She embraced him, her breasts rising in hot invitation against his chest. "We know so little of each other."

"But we learn more each day and night." He traced the frilly line of her ear. "I know you are a widow who has lost her husband and her child. A sorrow that still stings. I know you see my Bella as the sweet child she is. But I also know you desire me and give yourself with an abandon that fills my soul with gratitude. Come for a picnic today with Bella, my sister, and her beau, Langley, too."

"I'd be happy to."

For once, she did not argue. He rejoiced at the small victory. "Noon, then?"

"I must leave after an hour."

He cocked a brow, teasing her with a wariness he, happily, did not feel. "An engagement with another man?"

"There is no other man."

He threaded his fingers through her long, silken waves. "I'm very glad to hear that."

"Is there another woman?" Her words held fear, but also in her expression was a distaste for her arrogance to ask.

"No. Not for the longest time."

She swallowed hard. "Why is that?"

"I've been waiting to be enchanted by you."

She took the compliment with a grin and hugged him, her glorious hair trailing down her back into his palms. "I like picnics. Little sandwiches and cakes. Grass and sky. A kite."

He grinned. "And you."

Her lips parted, her blue eyes limpid with tears.

He inhaled, fighting for sanity. "I must stop kissing you."

"Then I will kiss *you*." She laughed and blessed his mouth with that sweet caress of hers.

He was lost to her, in her. Such bliss he'd never known.

Only when she fell back to the bed, once more exhausted with their mutual climax, did he shake himself to leave. He gathered his determination just as he gathered his clothes from the floor and took them into her sitting room to don.

Before him stood her easel with a panoramic sketch of the Brighton waterfront. The candles that had burned as they made love had guttered. The light in the room was dim. But dawn broke. He could see her work. A glimpse told him she was talented. Another told him she worked at perfect depiction of the elevation of buildings to seashore.

The longer he stared at it, the more he frowned.

He'd visited this seacoast town so often for business and pleasure since childhood that he immediately recognized the scope, from the eastern fringes to the newer developments to the west.

His darling lady was talented. An expert landscaper, she had the skills of an expert draftsman.

He was buttoning his waistcoat as he felt her arms go around his chest. He turned to embrace her tightly to him. She'd wore a diaphanous wrap that felt like cream beneath his fingertips.

Drowsy, she lifted her face to his. "This was no escapade."

He put his lips to hers in a gentle kiss. "Not for me either. Let me go, my darling. I will return. I promise. Noon."

"Noon." She looped her arm through his and led him to her door.

Chapter Thirteen

"**Y**OU SLEPT LATE," Clive's sister commented as she poured him a second cup of coffee from her breakfast service in her rooms.

"I did. Thank you." He strolled with his cup and saucer to the window. He knew what Terese was about to say.

"Is this"—she waved a hand—"wise?"

"Infatuation is never wise." He dared not call it love. Not aloud. Perhaps soon he could shout it to anyone, because the feeling pulsed like a potent promise in every fiber of his being.

"I do agree with that," she said. "Many noticed that you and Giselle departed early."

He took a drink and shook his head. His sister was not angry, nor did she really care what society thought or rumored. But she was careful of his emotions, proud of his status and his work, honest to a fault when it came to discussing their challenges with others.

"There was nothing for it, Terese. I wanted her. She cares for me."

"Well then, I think we must make her more welcome. Shall we have her to luncheon?"

"I have invited her to a picnic and to sail kites at noon. I hope Langley will come."

"I'm sure he will."

He faced his perceptive sister. "I do adore you, Terese. You are my bulwark and my confidante. How you help with Bella. Here. In London. Now with this…this." He stared into his coffee. "I feel oddly light, as if I am fifteen."

She shivered in her chair. "A bit of a tingle to be in love and fifteen, yes?"

Clive knew once she had been in love recklessly. When she was seventeen, she announced to their father that she would wed the new young gardener on their country estate. Their sire had ended that with the announcement that she would wed a man he chose. Terese packed a bag and ran south to her swain. She did not get far, only to Maidstone, before their father's men hauled her back to London. She was married the next month to a man twice her age. But the two of them had found love, even if it was short lived. The loneliness of widowhood did not sit well with her. However, she'd never lost her good humor or her hope for a better future. If she had hoped for a better mate, she'd found none for years. When she helped Clive get through his own loveless marriage and its disappointments, she had helped to save his sanity and right his thinking.

He had no compunction about asking the next thing of her. "Advise me on this, please, Terese."

"Oh, darling brother of mine, I am no authority on such matters. I find love before me once again and marvel at the apparition. I can impart nothing but how blissful it is to find it."

Clive stilled at the thought he might be truly in love. "Terese, I am thirty-four. I am too old to fall for a lady so quickly." *Aren't I?*

"Age and time are qualifiers of desire?"

More than that is my niggling sense that something is very wrong with those paintings of hers. "I don't know. I cannot believe I spent the night…" He left off the rest. It would be indelicate to indicate the hours he'd spent making love to Giselle Laurant three times.

Terese chuckled. "Clive, really. You are not the first person to celebrate the honeymoon before the wedding."

"You assume I will marry her?"

His sister, two years his senior, was educated, temperate, and just the finest, jolliest person. She saw wise men for what they offered the world…and called out all fools for what they assumed was theirs to command.

"I leave that to your discretion, my dear. I'd say to be careful. If she is for you, then each time you meet, the love will grow and never falter."

"No matter logic or doubts."

"No matter."

⊁⟫⟫⟨⟨⊀

THEY WALKED TO a park west of the pavilion, Terese and Giselle arm in arm. Bella had her father's hand and chattered about the kite and the sweets she knew were in the hamper that Clive carried. Langley carried another smaller filled with juices. Along the path, Giselle noticed her new guard lingered not far off. As they chose a spot on a grassy knoll, the man took up a spot in the foliage of an old fir tree.

She shook off the feeling that someone else followed them. Her ugly stalker again? With so many around her, anyone would be foolish to try to harm her.

Langley was discussing marriage, and suddenly, Giselle realized he meant that he and Terese were about to be wed.

"Congratulations to you both," she offered. "I gather from your words that your plans are recently made?"

"Yesterday, Terese did me the honor of accepting my proposal. I'll return to London tomorrow to acquire a special license for us to marry soon." Langley lifted Terese's hand and kissed her fingers. "I'd say next week would be good, don't you?"

"You don't mind, do you, Clive, that the wedding will be so soon?" Terese asked.

"Not at all, my dear. You must please yourself," Clive replied.

"But you wanted to stay for another week here so that you and Bella would have a proper holiday."

"Terese, you have done so much for me, taking Bella every day so that I could work. Coming with me here to help with her. I could not refuse you anything in this world. All I ask is that you two do not wed without me there." Clive smiled with the affection of years of loving his kind sister.

"I can continue to be her loving aunt. I hope you will allow me to take her each day."

"Dearest," Clive said with a kind smile to Langley, "you will be assuming the role of wife to your new husband, ordering his house and becoming mother to his eight-year-old son. You will have so many new responsibilities, I cannot ask you to keep on with Bella."

"But I am not a young bride, Clive." Terese had an edge to her retort. "I know how to run a house, surely. I do not wish to give up the joy of Bella."

"I did not mean to anger you, Terese. I would not tear you two apart."

Langley reached over to take his fiancée's hand. "Neither would I. You come to me as my wife, Terese, I do hope, with all your desires assured. I would welcome Bella to come to us each day."

Terese shrugged her shoulders. "Very well. As long as we each understand that I am not abandoning who I was for who I will become."

Both men agreed.

"Forgive us, Giselle, as we settle our family issues in front of you," Terese added.

Giselle smiled at each in turn. "I am pleased to see a family who can solve their problems."

The warm regard that Giselle saw in each person's attitude toward the other inspired her anew. So few of her husband and her challenges were ever solved so quickly and without malice.

As she got to her feet and brushed off blades of grass from her skirts, Clive rose to help her up. "I think it is time to put this kite into the air. Bella!" he called to his daughter, who talked to herself as she plucked petals from wildflowers. "Come fly this new kite!"

GISELLE PLUNKED DOWN on the picnic blanket, winded from her run with Bella. Content, she watched Clive run the kite with his daughter. She grinned, more alive than she'd felt in years. The sun shone on her, Bella, Terese, Langley—and on her lover.

My lover.

She savored the words in her mind. The delicious man she'd discovered was worthy of a portrait by her friend Élisabeth. His light-brown hair streaked with blond, his shining gray eyes, his breadth, his depth of person, how she loved him.

Loved him.

The flames of her desire flared up, and she gazed at him with a yearning she knew not that she had ever possessed. Her mouth fell open at the admission to herself. She must not love him so much, so well, or she would endanger him. Bella, Terese. Who knew how many could fall to her enemies?

He looked over at her—and paused. As if he'd heard her thoughts, her fears. Perceptive man. He saw into her. Finishing her sentences. Understanding her before she had a chance to tell him all.

How was that?

In the village outside her papa's chateau near Blois, a gypsy woman had lived. She lived alone, her family long gone to some purge. But she remained, an infamous and yet valued resident.

Her father called the woman One-Eyed Esmeralda. But she saw with more than that one orb. She predicted Giselle's own marriage. "A selfish man will take you," Esmeralda had told her when she begged for a reading of her hand. "You will not like him, and he will take you for your flesh."

All of that had been true. Too accurate.

Esmeralda had also predicted her father's death by guillotine. "The razor," she'd said with a swipe of her fingers across her throat and sadness in her craggy face. Those in the village loved Giselle's father. "The Vicomte de Touraine," Esmeralda had said, "his like will never be seen here again."

"Have you been in England long? ...Giselle?" Terese leaned across their blanket to touch her hand. "Giselle?"

"*Je suis desole.*" Giselle straightened in her chair. "I...as you say here, gather silk."

Both Terese and Clive gave a laugh.

"That's wool," he said.

"Please repeat what you asked of me, Terese. I am enjoying the day."

"I wondered how long you had been in England," Terese said.

"Since last October."

Clive frowned. "That must have been difficult, what with the blockade."

"It was. Very." Giselle rubbed her arms, recalling the freezing journey. "I sailed from Ostend on a merchant's boat. He is a renegade from the French government and runs a business smuggling those like me out of France to Britain."

Terese murmured an epithet, then said, "How brave of you."

"It was necessary." Giselle hated to tell the story of her family's ruin, but these people before her were kind and loving. She had no reason to conceal who or what she had been.

"*Mon père*...my father, was the tenth Vicomte de Touraine. A supporter of the rights of man, he lived for a time in Versailles and advised the last king on reforms. They were, of course, too little, too late. But then it put him in Robespierre's sights. He escaped to Verdun and took my brother, my sister, and me with him. But we were discovered by the local *gendarmes* and sent back to Paris. My father ensured that my brother and I escaped the guards. He did not."

"Your sister escaped as well?" Terese asked.

"No. She was older than I. Lovely. Lively. Taken to the deputy of police, who put her in La Force when she would not consent to his affections. She died there."

"I am so sorry." Terese was rapt.

Clive was horrified. "And your mother?"

Giselle struggled to tell more. "*Ma mère* died the first year of the insurrection. She was a princess *du sang*, of the blood of the Valois, and feared for all of us. She had a weak heart. The fear killed her."

Terese took her hand and squeezed in sympathy. "My dear. That is all so heartrending to hear."

"And your brother?" Clive asked.

"He was recaptured and also taken to La Force. He argued publicly against the emperor. Fouché's deputy, René Vaillancourt—the same man who took my sister—arrested him more than a year ago."

"And you?" Clive stared at her intensely.

"He wanted me as well. I escaped him with the help of a few friends."

"I assume Vaillancourt has posted a ransom for your capture." Clive scowled, angry, bitter.

She met his gaze with fear eating her heart. "Five thousand Napoleons."

"Dear God." Terese sagged in horror.

"You must not go about alone." Clive leaned over and seized her hand. His affection stirred her memories of his tenderness last night.

"I know. I am skilled at escape, subterfuge. I move about."

"We can help you," Terese said with conviction.

"I do not wish to endanger your lives." Giselle's gaze swept from Terese, to Clive, and down to Bella. Clive and Terese gaped.

She had told them too much. They were appalled, and she had been silly to endanger them with her presence. Mad to fall in love with this charming gentleman. She had to go. Had to leave…leave *him*!

"I will help you." This from Clive had Giselle shaking her head.

"No! I would not see you hurt. None of you. I venture out carefully. I see no one today who would hurt me."

He moved closer on the blanket toward her. "I will be sore of heart if you do not permit me the honor of helping you."

She could not allow it. He would ruin her plans, perceive too much, and most likely misinterpret her work. She must not fail. Amber knew of the dangers she faced. So too did Gus. Their husbands as well. She had guards following her, hired by them. She knew them by sight. Clive would spot them and might perceive, if he did not already, who and what they were. "I have a plan. I will proceed with it, sir."

"Clive. My name is Clive, and you, my dear Giselle, must listen to me." He grabbed her hand.

"No, no! Do not do this. Do not box me in."

"Giselle—" Terese pleaded.

"Giselle," Clive persisted, "I'll take no refusals. I've heard reports of Vaillancourt. He is cunning. His men are notoriously ruthless. You cannot hold them off by sheer will alone."

Giselle shook him off and pushed to her feet. She would not be controlled. Not by Clive, the dashing, dear man who graced her bed last night. She endangered his life now. Oh, what a fool she had been. "Please. Heed me. I am determined and dedicated. I have my own means to deter Vaillancourt and all the French."

Then she marched away.

Clive followed. Coming right beside her, he caught her arm.

She shook him off.

"You do this, whatever it is, to get your brother free?"

"No." She grumbled to herself that he was most likely dead. No one lived long in La Force. "Go back to the picnic, Clive."

"Tell me what you do to get him free!"

"No."

"I can help you, darling. Let me."

"I will not endanger you. It was wrong to have become so intimate."

"Never, sweetheart." His words were so sincere, she paused to stare at him and dash a tear from her cheek. "I am yours now. And you are mine."

"That cannot be! Go away."

He grasped both her hands. "No!"

"Clive, stop." She shook back her hair, tormented that he might pay a price for caring for her. "I have plans. Friends. In the meantime, I work."

"Your work," he mused, his voice dropping to an ominous tone. "Whatever it is, you must tell me later."

A lady approached along the walk.

Giselle bent closer to him. "Never, my dear man. You would be a target of my foes. I would never do that." She straightened her spine and found cold words to repel him. "Thank you for the picnic. I did enjoy your company. Goodbye, Clive."

HER REPUDIATION ROILED him. How dare she think he would abandon her to Vaillancourt, to *anyone* who would hurt her? She had good reason for this work she did, and he was damned if he'd let her do it alone. She did not want him near her? Well, she was mistaken if she thought he was so lacking in creativity.

He stopped momentarily and ran a hand through his hair.

Then he took a few long strides to catch up to her. He did not approach. She did not stop. When she got to the hotel, she hiked her skirts and ran up the steps at a jog.

Once she disappeared safely inside, he stood on the corner collecting his thoughts. He'd arranged a man to follow her. Today at the picnic, he'd detected a man overly curious about their party's actions. He prayed to God that was his man.

But I am not certain, and the only way to assure myself of her safety is to be by her side.

Become her lover again. Her guard, her protection. Show her how he cared so much that he would let no one harm her.

He'd ask Terese to take Bella with her to London tomorrow. An imposition, yes, but he was certain Terese would not only see the challenge here, but agree he had to act. Also, he'd write to Mr. and Mrs. Campbell, who staffed his cottage east of here. He'd ask them to stock the little house—and tell no one that they had heard from him.

Whatever your work, my darling, you'll do it in the safety of my house and my arms.

$$\text{Chapter Fourteen}$$

GISELLE STOOD BACK to examine the last stroke on the small houses of Hove. Those buildings to the west of the center of Brighton were only a few, the population of Hove perhaps two or three hundred. The Bath stone of the more muscular houses was a slightly creamier shade of that found in older buildings in the city center. The rest were of brick. They provided the picture of the shore so necessary to her work.

She removed the clip that pinned the stock to the back of her easel and took it to her window. Pulling back the lace curtain, she raised the thick paper to the sunlight. Yes, she approved of this one. Only another morning and she would finish this. Then she could begin the east side of town.

She frowned.

It was the part of Brighton she knew least. She had not walked there at all, but this afternoon she had reason. She was to meet Jacques Durand's new man and tell him she'd have his final drawings to convey to Durand to take across the Channel.

She pushed down her questions about this morning and this new man employed by the one who had smuggled her across the sea. Durand, notorious and wanted by the British and French governments, did a service for the Crown. Running goods like cognac and schnapps, china and carpets through the tight shipping lines, Durand also smuggled those who wished to escape the claws of Napoleon. She had sailed with him, terror struck and chilled to the bone, but rejoiced to land alive and well. Now she would send back tomorrow with his man the last of the drawings she'd been recruited to do. This set would complement those other, smaller versions that Lord Ramsey had managed to put into suspected French agents' hands. Much like the set in Hastings that were to be purchased, so it was believed, by a French spy, this set for Durand would confirm the seascape, its elevation, and its surrounding buildings. Proud of all her work, she thrilled to hear the end was near.

The victory came with bittersweet regret. She had sacrificed for it greatly. Clive Davenport, her dashing lover, had not bothered her at all these past three days. He had followed her back to the hotel that day after she abruptly left the picnic. But he had not knocked on her door nor sent a message to her. He most likely had returned to London with his daughter, his sister, and Lord Langley. Better for it, too, he was, out of danger and done with the heartbreak she could not avoid causing him.

As for her own grinding loss of him, she shoved that ache down, down, down as deep as it would go. Soon she would deal with that…and surrender to that grief which she knew might well kill her.

After her work was completed in a few days and sent off with Durand's man across the waters to Boulogne, she would go west to Cornwall. The image she held in her mind of wild winds and lightning crashing on a rugged shore spoke to her current belief that chaos reigned over a damaged world. Her brief affair with Clive had shown her vistas painted in rolling greens and scudding blues brilliant with a golden sun.

Gone now.

Dissolved in the mists of yesterday.

AN HOUR LATER, she stood outside the blacksmith's shop. Durand's man was late.

For safety, she'd arrived in a hired hack. But as few walked the street, she took the liberty to do so herself. Strolling down the street, she noted the dimensions of the bakery and the bookstore next to it. The shops along this part of the eastern promenade were tiny compared to those in the Lanes near the pavilion. She would render them as they truly were.

She walked back to her meeting point. As she went, she reevaluated her original calculations of length of street, heights of buildings, and the depth of the beach from sea to seawall. Her method of calculation corresponded to her length of stride. She'd done it so often, her actions were automatic. She stood a moment and paced off in her mind the distance from the smithy to the shoreline.

She flexed her shoulders and scanned the street once more. It was noon, but few were about. She could wonder why, but credited it to the sticky weather. Too hot for June, the air suddenly seemed to smother her.

She checked the watch pinned to the collar of her pelisse. She'd wait only for another ten minutes, then be gone. He would have to make another appointment, because she would not risk waiting too long. She suspected that anyone observing her now would question her intentions. Did she meet a friend? Did she have a rendezvous with a lover?

She scoffed. *If only.*

She began to pace.

ACROSS THE CORNER, Clive sat by the window, tracking her movements.

"Another, milord?" The barmaid hoisted a stone pitcher of beer.

"Aye, thank you." He sat back to allow her access to pour.

The woman bent to follow his line of sight through the window. "Pretty lady. Yours?"

What to say, other than, "I hope so."

She wrinkled her nose in distaste. "A man came earlier today and walked that corner."

"When did he leave?" Clive had no idea if what they spoke of was of any importance, but he'd research every fact if it meant he would save Giselle from whatever and whomever she feared.

The maid shrugged. "Maybe…eleven?"

"I see. What did he look like?"

"Gruff. No shave. Rough and dirty, hair like string."

"His nose?"

The woman gave a start, looked at Clive with a smirk, and said, "Flat."

"Ah." So not the beak-nosed one, but a colleague, perhaps. *Christ, what a tangle.*

"But there's another one. Look. He likes the looks of your lady. He's going to stop her, seems like."

The stranger charged toward her.

In a snap, Clive was up out of his chair, his coin on the table. "Thank you."

He was just crossing the street when Giselle spied him.

She gasped and spun sway. Right into Mister Flat Nose's open arms.

"Bugger." Clive slid his stiletto from his waistcoat pocket.

But the man was fast, coiling his arm around Giselle's throat and dragging her back toward the lean-to of the blacksmith's shop.

"Let her go," Clive seethed as he marched in time with him.

The man sneered and flicked a small knife against Giselle's ear. "Don't try."

"She's mine," Clive spat. "You haven't a chance."

"No?" The cur yanked her backward.

Her eyes wide upon Clive, she pleaded with him for reprieve.

'Twas then Clive's own hired man slithered from the shadows of the blacksmith's shop and took the fellow down the same way he'd tried to fell Giselle.

"Shall I skin 'im, sir?" His man's evil grin showed crooked black teeth.

Clive took Giselle's wrists and pulled her to him. "Learn who pays him. I don't care how. Send me word via the hotel. Come, sweetheart. We leave these two to their urgent business."

Chapter Fifteen

GISELLE SQUIRMED IN her seat. She and Clive had ridden for at least an hour in a traveling coach he had hired from some stables somewhere in Brighton. Minutes ago at a crossroads, they had switched to another carriage.

She did not ask for details. She was too angry, too frightened, and, frankly, too grateful to him to care. She crossed her arms, stared out the window, and relived over and over the horror of that man trying to…what? Kill her? Abduct her? Make her give him her drawings?

She'd never know.

Meanwhile, she faced Clive. Furious with her, he did not speak, nor reprimand her. A good thing. She would have given his frustration back to him.

Where they went was her primary thought. He had a plan but did not share it. So be it. She could accept it for now.

Suppressing a sigh, she realized she still had work to do. She eyed the pile of stock that he and she had collected from her room. Her drawings were all there. She would not leave without them. Her small oils and watercolors were in her work satchel in the boot. Her clothes, too, were there. His as well. They'd packed in a frenzy, calling for no maids or footmen to help, lest they ask where or why they left so quickly.

Wherever Clive took her now, she had one problem—how to finish her drawings of Brighton and deliver them to Durand's accomplice. She had no idea how to find the smuggler's man. He would always contact her so that she could hand over her drawings. If he had any idea of what had happened to her, she did not know. Could not discover.

She grumbled. What a coil!

But she would find a way. She would. She was nearly done with her work, and Clive Davenport could save her from a kidnapper, spirit her away, and offer her safety. But he would not stop her.

She loved him. His care of her. His devotion to her welfare. His ingenuity.

He could not stop her.

SHE SEARED HIM with her anger. Too bad. Did she think he'd blithely watch as she was abducted? Or worse?

He had a plan. It was working. He'd asked for secrecy from the hotel receptionist to hire a coach. Then he had ordered that coachman to take them to another posting inn where they could easily switch to another carriage. Yes, they traveled in broad daylight, but there was nothing for it. They had to leave Brighton and do it immediately.

Thank God he'd written days ago to his caretakers of his cottage. The Campbells were attentive and always at the ready to receive him. He had not visited often and had even offered the cottage to his friends and associates when they were in need. Recently, the man who took residence had done so because he had abducted the lady he loved...and done so by mistake.

This act, to take Giselle, was certainly no mistake. He sat back, nodding at the familiar bend in the road that would take them to the little thatched-roof cottage where he had grieved the demise of his unfortunate marriage at the death of his wife.

The coach turned south onto a great road, and he spied the small house that sat near the rocks of the beach. This was his caretakers' home. Farther up the lane along a verdant forest path stood the cottage he and Giselle were to inhabit.

There was everything they needed. Supplied with food and whisky, they could live here indefinitely. The Campbells, the jolly older couple whom he had employed more than ten years ago, would see to their welfare.

What he and Giselle needed most was time to finish whatever work she had left—and to heal this breach between them.

If she would allow it.

His gaze drifted to her stack of watercolor drawings on the seat beside her. That was what kept them apart.

He had to persuade her to tell him what she did and why she could die because of it. He thought he had figured out her goal, but he had learned long ago never to predict and never to presume to know the workings of anyone's heart.

She could have died in Brighton.

He would not allow it.

He would help her.

No matter how she argued.

$$\text{Chapter Sixteen}$$

THEIR DAYS IN Clive's lovely, quaint cottage were quiet, peaceful—and tense. Their nights, sleeping separately in the alcove off the great room, were a torment. He would lie on his side facing her, his gray eyes upon her until she fell asleep, his eyes open and staring at her when she awakened.

They spoke rarely, only out of necessity.

Did he want her to cook him oats for breakfast?

Did she wish to go with him down to the sea for a stroll or a swim?

Would she like another cognac?

Could she have his small things, please, to do the wash?

Giselle wished for more ease between them. It came one night when Clive began to laugh at a book he read.

"Will you read aloud to me?" she asked him, eager for the mellifluous sound of his deep voice to fill the soft night air and calm her weary heart.

When he did, she fell asleep in her chair. The next morning, she awoke in her bed, snuggled in blankets, fully dressed.

Clive Davenport was an ethical man who filled her soul with longing.

She covered her desires with activity.

When she wasn't at her easel, she was in the kitchen. Each

morning, Mrs. Campbell brought them beautiful baskets of fresh-picked winter turnips, potatoes, spring lettuces, radishes, cucumbers, and a few early tomatoes. Admiring the wealth of vegetables in the wicker basket, Giselle let her memory fly back to her youth, when she spent hours in her parents' kitchen. And later in her own, she had continued when she sought solitude and safety from her demanding and often cruel husband. Just as in art, she controlled what she created. She could walk into a fantastical cloud of transforming simple ingredients into mouth-watering delicacies—and get lost.

With flour, eggs, and cream, Giselle made flan. With cherries, she made a cake so light and sweet, she had tears in her eyes at the memory of such a cake she'd made for her father.

She whipped eggs to a froth as if she stirred the winds over the earth. She molded pie shells into elegant shapes of flowers and animals, baked them to a pretty golden brown with apples or pears or raisins and dates melding together in heady aromas and sinfully tasty treats. They had honey cakes and smooth breads.

One day she decided to tackle her favorite pastry. Years ago in Blois, she had devoted herself to making a confection of a thousand layers dripping with thick cream and ganache. It had taken her months of trial and error, remeasuring and calculations, but she had triumphed and conquered the pastry. Now, with success in hand from the simpler dishes she made, she tried again on the *millefeuille*.

It took her eleven days to get it right. Finished with her work for the day, she would take up the recipe. Her hair slipping from her pins, her cheeks dotted with flour, her lips covered in sugars, she was happy to serve Clive her wares each night, even if she'd not yet perfected the recipe.

Clive—good man, his mouth full, eyes widened or rolling in ecstasy—could barely find words to describe how he loved the various forms of the delicacy. She would preen, tickled that she progressed in its creation, thrilled at his delight in it.

She did justice, too, to other treats that Mrs. Campbell

brought them. A leg of lamb Giselle studded with garlic and fresh herbs. The roast filled the little cottage with the aromas that denoted springtime and renewal. She made potato fritters and pork cutlets. Cabbage slaws with carrots. Stews of beans and onions with beef or chicken. Each new dish filled her with pride. Clive filled her with compliments.

He became her assistant. Taking instruction from her, he'd wash the vegetables, measure flour and sugar, and even learned how to slice on the diagonal to preserve flavor. What she produced stunned him with the flavors and variety—and he told her so without end.

One week later, Mrs. Campbell, cheery soul, had brought round the morning's freshly picked lettuce, spinach, and onions. Bright-red strawberries too came from somewhere close by. Giselle did not ask for details. She settled her hands on her hips and thought of how she could make a meal from the produce.

"A feast," Clive said as he came to stand behind her in the little alcove that served as their small kitchen. His warmth flowed into her from his attitude and his words. The fragrance of his cologne filled her lungs with a desire to turn and kiss their conflict away.

"I think so," she told him, and wished to give him in return the peace he engendered. What little she had to offer was another of her skills in the art of cooking. "A salad for lunch. For dinner, the potatoes and onions, a bit of cream to make a pie."

"I can peel the potatoes for you."

She had taught him how yesterday. He was always ready to help, but at this, he was all thumbs. She had teased him that he might well use his long, sharp Italian blade and do a better job. He'd given her a sidelong glance and said he'd use it better to stick a potato on the end and roast it. She had to smile at that, and he noticed, his mellow gaze dropping to her lips.

She licked her lower lip.

He imitated her.

She spun away. "Mr. Campbell is late this morning." The

man usually came around ten. The sun had long been up. "You don't suppose something is wrong, do you?"

"We are secluded here, Giselle. Campbell probably has an errand. He will come and I will go out for my patrol."

He went three to four times a day, taking his pistol and his nasty stiletto. Mr. Campbell stayed with Giselle as Clive did his rounds. But at all other times, the man kept watch from his and his wife's cottage down the lane. Clive and his man had devised a schedule so that each saw the other pass in view at least once an hour.

Giselle felt the security like a balm to her fears. She was succumbing to the charms of ordinary pleasures. And of Clive.

DESPITE NEVER HAVING anyone to talk with about what she did or why, she still did not wish to start now. Except to share her thoughts with Clive. That, she recognized, was how her love for him changed her. But she ignored it and turned to her work and her cooking. Clive said little to disturb her or distract her.

She held her tongue. Held her breath. Soon she would be finished with her work. Finished here with him. And leave.

The prospect began to tear at her. No drawing, no cooking could tame her anxiety. She feared for her contact, Jacques Durand's man. She did not sleep well. During the day, she kept in constant motion. Her work, her cooking, her obsession with contemplating whatever had happened to the various men who had tracked her or those who had protected her. Then one day, worn to a frazzle by her fruitless worry, it vanished.

She let it all go.

She still wished for a way to communicate with the Ashleys or Ramseys from here. She could not risk the mail. Did not have enough coin to hire a messenger. Nor could she even find one. No one came to their cottage but the Campbells.

From the beginning of her work here along the Channel, she'd understood she worked alone. Never afraid for her safety until Durand's man had not appeared outside the Old Ship and other, more devious-looking men began to pop up, she was grateful for the protection Clive offered. Another reason to appreciate his spontaneity with her cooking; another reason to marvel at his generosity. Another reason to love him.

And because she had to leave him, those were also good reasons why she must never tell him so.

PRECIOUS.

That was the only word she could think of to describe her days and nights with him. He lured her with quiet acquiescence to her needs. With his easy offer to help her cook or clean, his hearty laugh, or his recognition that here in this cottage they were friends, walking around each other carefully. By her preoccupation with all else, save him, she told him they could not sleep together. That she would not approach him to make it so.

They were here for a reason that had a beginning and an ending, as chilling as it was dispassionate. By keeping his distance, he seemed to have silently agreed that their desire for each other was an emotion from another time, another place, another realm. None of which would ever be theirs again. Yet between them in the quiet hours, when she sat opposite him after dinner and before she retired to her bed alone, she knew she could claim him as hers forever if she just crossed to him and forgot her purpose and lived for the moment.

Despite her devotion to her own cause, she felt the promise of what might have been as, throughout each new day, her gaze drifted toward him. She would watch him read, his firm lips pressed into an appealing line. She could trace the outline of his jaw, square and strong, his beard heavy. From that night they'd spent entangled in each other, she recalled his whiskers against her cheek. They were soft, brushing her senses with his heat.

She'd shake her head and go back to her book of poetry. But heavens. She knew the lines by heart. There were few books in this cottage, and the poetry seemed the only one upon the shelf that could entertain her. Except when it didn't. And Clive Davenport was the only person she ever wished to read. Bored as she was with the bad poems, pretending fascination was not her skill. Her eyes, rebellious and needy, would close, open, and seek out the beauty of him.

He filled her gaze, her mind, her heart tumbling over with praise for what he was. What he did for her.

Smart man, he would meet her regard with those large gray orbs—and hold. First came his flash of delight that she watched him, the corners of his eyes crinkling in the fleeting joy. Then a searing desire would narrow his gaze upon her and burn its way into her tormented heart.

She had no alternative but to hurry to her cold and lonely bed.

PROXIMITY BROUGHT HIM insight.

Clive poured two short glasses of cognac. They had just finished their dinner, a feast of fresh flounder sautéed in butter and topped with crab. His darling was a fabulous cook. Their meals these past three weeks had been the very best he'd ever eaten.

So too had their companionship become easier. She did not talk much as she pored over her drawings. Mumbled to herself, yes, about this stroke or that. The color was too deep. The tone too heavy. She'd correct each little bit.

Watching her work, putting together what he knew, he also understood what he needed to do. What he needed to draw from her. When a child, he'd been a keen student of his father's knowledge of the sea, the tides, the moon and stars. He'd been at his work for the Foreign Office for three years. A contentious marriage and a need to contribute what he could had sent him to offer his services. His knowledge of the southern shore had been useful to Secretary Mulgrave, but also to Halsey and the prime minister.

They had discussed with local officials the needs and improvements for fortifications along the coastal towns and villages. They had consulted with the navy and the army about deployment of troops, ships, and supplies. They had determined what kind of timing was necessary if Bonaparte attacked here or there. Or if he came by hot air balloon, a tunnel under the Channel, upon amphibious craft, or by ship, they calculated how to repel him. They had estimated how quickly he might land troops, gain control over British forces, how quickly he could put in fresh troops for those wounded or killed. They had estimated under any scenario how quickly the Frenchman might resupply his men with rifles, food, and shelter.

Now, nine months since Mulgrave, Halsey, and Clive had begun their own plan of coastal defense, they waited with bated breath for a sign—any sign—that the two hundred thousand men of the Grande Armée were ready to go to sea. He had heard them—who had not?—rallying from Boulogne, their wild *huzzahs* carrying to England on the winds. He had read reports from his three agents in Normandy that they drilled night and day. Bonaparte had tightened their ranks, the regiments filled with experts in attack, defense, maneuver, and some new strategic movement called the wheel.

The emperor had also reorganized the structure of each regiment. Within each were paymasters, engineers, scouts, and experts of all types. Independence from other regiments thus ensured that any segment cut from another by choice or chance would continue efficiently until reunited with the rest. Thus, their integrity assured for a short or long time, the soldiers of the armies of France could go proud and confident to battle. Whether they went confident to sea was a question unanswered in Clive's mind.

That was not a matter he could settle tonight with Giselle. But he could bring to a head the question of her work. He'd nurtured for weeks grave suspicions of what she did. Now that he had a closer look each day, he assured himself that his conclusions were sound ones. But he would no longer live in the dark, allowing her any quarter that she was free or right or capable of enacting this charade on her own. He would demand she tell him what she did. Perhaps even why.

He watched her as she went to the bed beyond the great room wall. As she did each night after supper, she took down her midnight hair and let it curl about her shoulders and her firm, generous breasts. Then she brushed the waves to a shine. Tonight, he had no intention of allowing her to end the day and easily elude him by climbing into bed.

He would have answers. He would have closure.

His gaze on the way her hands stroked her hair over her shoulder burned with new urgency. "Come talk with me, Giselle."

Her long lashes flickered, but her eyes met his. "I am tired."

"As am I. Of so much. Come. Drink with me." He indicated the two whisky glasses on the table to his side. "Please."

She'd removed her muslin gown, her petticoat, and, as far as he could tell, her chemise as well. Days ago, she'd given up her corset. The curve of her breasts in her gowns had transformed him into a ghoul of desire. He'd allowed himself to look at her only above her chin. Now his gaze devoured every inch of curves. He snatched his reason and crushed it close to his heart—and planned his next words.

She came forward, her robe of translucent pink silk billowing around her form and the more modest translucent white muslin night rail. As her gaze sank into his, he saw her understanding of the severity of his intent.

She took the overstuffed chair next to his and picked up one glass.

"My apologies. It's Scotch, not French cognac," he said as he raised his glass to his lips. "Campbell could not get another bottle of the cognac."

"It will do." She drank, closed her eyes as she swallowed, then sighed. "More than. It's very smooth."

"You are nearly finished with the sketches of Brighton."

"I think they are complete." Her blue eyes locked on his, her request for honesty bold. "Do you agree?"

That last he appreciated. She'd predicted his knowledge of the shore. "The eastern sector of the town needs a bit more definition. But otherwise, yes. It is well done."

A ghost of a smile of satisfaction curved her plump lips. She considered the whisky in her tumbler.

"So then." He swirled the liquid in his glass. "My father was in the Royal Navy. A captain, at last rank when he was wounded in the siege of Charleston in '80. Minus his left eye, he returned home. His older brother died soon after, and my father inherited the title and the estate. He lived, often in pain that made him grind his teeth. Yet he found great joy from my mother, who loved him dearly, and from Terese and me, rascal that I was.

"Each spring, he would take us to Brighton. He bought a small sloop, moored it there. He would take us out each day, sometimes twice. He taught me about tides and wind, how to fish and how to sail his precious, one-masted little boat. I was never a sailor. I like the sea, but could not live there. I prefer land and stability and the grit of soil under my fingernails.

"Of all the cities and towns along the Channel, I know Brighton best. Of French towns, I've often been to Le Havre and Calais. Once during the Peace of Amiens three years ago, I traveled to Dieppe. I understand the lay of the seascape. I have seen the plains of Boulogne and I understand why Bonaparte sent his army there to train and to frighten us."

Giselle had listened patiently to his words. But in this lull, she nodded, appreciating the story of his life. "I have watched you examine my sketches and watercolors. I know you search for what I do."

Grateful she had said that, he grew bold to move onward. "I no longer search, Giselle. I know. I see it plainly. What's more, I have inklings of how you wish to use these drawings to their purpose."

"Clive," she whispered, curling her shoulders about her delicate frame, "you know I cannot tell you all."

"All?" Once that would have angered him. Now, he would take her along to his own conclusions. "You must tell me now if there is a need for all."

She set her teeth. "I do not wish you hurt."

"As a measure of how you care for me, yes, I take that. As an indication of how you are involved in something nefarious, I understand that, too."

She tipped up her chin. "I remain your friend."

"When we met, you told me you were not my enemy. I believed you."

"I thought so."

He would not be pacified by small truths. He needed the bigger ones. "I have seen you with your friends. The Ashleys and Ramseys are more than fond of you. They know you. You have met them publicly and, I venture to say, privately, too. I know both couples work for Scarlett Hawthorne, the merchant in the City who has more ties to the Continent than we in the government could ever count. You work for them."

Her lashes fluttered closed.

"You do. And these," he said as he waved an arm toward her easel and her stacks of work lined up upon the wooden floor, "these are your contribution to the defeat of Bonaparte. That drawing of Brighton is so false. The seawall is shorter in your drawing than it actually is. The breakwater is positioned farther west than in reality. The elevation of the beach is lower. You make these illustrations to delude the French."

She set her jaw and met his gaze straight on. "I do," she whispered.

He waited for the rest of her explanation. He was not moving until she gave him all.

She picked at the ripples of silk in her lap, then locked her gaze on his. "I learned how to draw and paint when I was young. Madame Le Brun and her friends were friends of my mother, and they were kind to me. Indulgent and sweet.

"As I grew older, I perfected my art. Before I married, I had commissions from two book publishers in the Rue du Bac in Paris for maps for travel books. I made some money and a good reputation. When I was forced to marry, my husband made me stop. He did not wish for a wife who challenged him in any way.

"When he died and his protection, such as it was, ended, I went to my old friends, Augustine and Amber. Lady Ashley and Lady Ramsey now. They were as opposed to the new regime as I, and they devised a way for me to contribute to the cause of Bonaparte's defeat."

"How long have you been doing this for them?"

"Working for Scarlett Hawthorne? More than two years, first as a runner, then later doing drawings. I took an old map I drew for a French travel book and approached one of Fouché's men."

"Vaillancourt?"

She shook her head. "No. His assistant. I had heard too much from Gus and Amber about the canny nature of Fouche's deputy, and I did not wish to tangle with him. My husband had dealings with Vaillancourt and lost. So I thought if I could influence one of his subordinates, I would do better. I did."

"I don't understand why you would take such a risk."

She rose and paced before him. "What had I to lose? My parents were dead. My father killed for politics. My sister gone. My brother gone, too, for his own views. Sent to prison by none other than Vaillancourt. My livelihood was gone, the vineyard fallow. My staff killed by those who would have total power.

"I had to leave France. I could not bear the fear that they would come for me. They had taken my older sister and abused her. I heard many gruesome stories of how guards in the prisons used women and destroyed them. I'd had enough of that rash and cruel behavior from my husband. I could not bear the thought of going to a cell or guards or rape. Call me a coward."

He cursed softly. "Never are you that."

"Still...still..." She crossed her arms and shuddered. "I could not live every day with the possibility they would take me away to starve me or...or rape me. I nearly lost my mind at home, awake each night in terror. I could not go on." She hung her head. "I would have gone mad if they took me."

She whirled to face him, her eyes envisioning horrors he could not see. "I had one skill. I could use it. So I fled to Paris. I approached a man, an Italian, who still works there for Scarlett Hawthorne. When Lord Ashley lived in Paris during the peace, this man was his majordomo. He helped Ashley keep order and expand his network of spies.

"I knew Corsini well. He helped me escape the country, pointing me toward a man who smuggles people and goods in and out of France."

Clive inhaled, satisfied finally to have the fuller explanation of her life. He'd take up this matter of her abusive husband in another way, another time. He'd not let her live with that as the template of how a man and woman should treat each other. He would move to his conclusion. "So now you have finished these last renderings of Brighton. We are here. So how did you plan to get them to your French smuggler?"

Her blue gaze dwelled on his, her hand clutching her diaphanous robe to her throat. "I would one day find a way to escape from you."

His heart thundered in his chest. "And run where?"

"Back to Brighton. To the hotel. To wait for a message from someone who would place a few in French agents' hands here in England or smuggle them back to France."

"You had a man following you."

"Hired by Ashley. He was my guard."

"I hired another to follow you."

"And there may have been yet another..." she said with a frown.

"You did not recognize any of them?"

"One man, ugly he was. With a beak nose, quite noticeable. Otherwise, I saw no one with any consistency. I was befuddled." Triumph flashed across her face. "But that man who appeared in east Brighton at just the right moment was yours. Thank you. I have not thanked you. I should have."

"You have no need to run from me."

She raised her head to examine the wooden rafters. "I wish that were so. You've heard my tale. You know I must deliver these last drawings and paintings. It is my satisfaction. My revenge on them all. That is if, of course, the French take them all to heart and calculate incorrectly how to land here."

He rose and went to her. Lifting her chin with two fingers, he traced her lower lip with his thumb. In his hands she turned sweet and soft. "You and I will return to Brighton. We'll take two suites at the hotel, but I will be with you night and day."

Acceptance had her swaying into him, and in her gaze stood joy in equal parts with fear. "I don't want you hurt."

"You know that the French will not stop hunting you."

"Whoever it is that suspects what I do, they can try to stop me. But my work is done."

"If Fouché and Vaillancourt know what you do for us, they will not stop." He would not reveal what he knew about the amphibious land craft. He had no confirmation from Langley or Halsey that the French calculations of the landing levers were made because of Giselle's art. If he told her, he'd frighten her more. "I want you with me every moment."

She flowed into his arms of her own accord, and Clive folded her close. "I want to be with you."

"Do you, my darling?" He crushed her near. "I am so very glad to hear that. I want you with me always."

She shook back her hair and gazed up at him. "You are too kind. I am no woman to match the valiant promise of you."

"I SAY YOU are more than that."

He growled and seized her lips in a kiss so hard, so deep, so fierce, she had no breath, no will but to claim more. She ran her fingers up through the soft hair over his ear, her other hand clutching his open shirt collar.

He broke away, catching air and considering the wall behind her. For a moment, she thought he'd stop.

But no. He cradled her head in his palms and, with some inscrutable words, took her mouth again.

This kiss was tender. The next wild.

She whimpered at the beauty of his claiming.

He crushed her closer, picking her up off her feet to match her frame to his torso.

With a shake of his head, he bent, then caught her up in his arms and strode like a conqueror to her bed.

He laid her down as if she were light as air and climbed over her. Up on his elbows, he hovered above. "Tell me to stop and I will."

How rare to find a man so considerate that he would offer to leave her. She cupped his cheeks. "I cannot. Tonight, I live for this. For you."

"For you," he murmured as if he said a prayer.

With one kiss of hard agreement, he rose on his knees and stripped his shirt over his head. In the flickering flames of the great room candles, she noted the breadth of his shoulders, the bulging muscles of his arms, the sharp ridges of his ribs. She traced them, drawing him in her heated mind. One day, she would paint him, sketch him, dashing man that he was. But tonight, she would love him as he deserved to be.

Her fingers slid to the buttons of his flies. She undid one, and he shot up and away, peeling off everything, even his boots, and pulling her to a sitting position.

Done in a second with her negligee and silly muslin gown, she lay naked before him. He ran his open palm from the hollow beneath her chin to her throat, her cleavage, and the point of one hard nipple and the other.

He swallowed so hard that she heard him as he returned to loom above her. She did the same to him as he had her and learned the contours of his shoulders, chest, and hips with her fingertips.

"Come to me," she whispered, arching her hips to his in invitation. "I need you. I have for all my life."

He gasped, his eyes at once full of tears. He dropped his head to catch her nipple in his mouth and suck her hard.

She bucked and dug her nails into his back.

He captured her other nipple and licked her until she keened. This, from him, was what love was like in heaven. Never had she had such on earth. And so she rose, one arm flung around his neck, one hand open, stroking the lean arc of his loins to his erect penis. There she wrapped her hand around him. Her hand was small compared to the enormous size of him, and she stroked him as if in compensation. He groaned and seated himself so that he ran his long member along her cleft. His fingers followed, and he opened her folds to murmur, "How wet and warm you are."

She shifted, and he dropped inside her, filling her with all of his flesh and devotion.

There he simply held.

"You are," he said, "so soft, so strong. Let me make you mine."

She gave a laugh that was half sob. "Do. Please."

At that, he slid his hands under her, one at her lower back, one at her hips. Then, with slow ardor she had known all too briefly weeks ago, he opened for her his gift of ecstasy that only love conveyed.

Nor was it done in a moment, but long, hot minutes of sensation, and at the end, hot, pounding release that shook her and took her far from the night, the bed, and left her with her arms full of him and a joy she'd never conceived that might be hers.

Chapter Seventeen

“I WILL MISS your excellent cooking,” Clive said as he settled across from her on his seat and the coach ground forward.

What she missed would be the passion and peace of the last few days. In his embrace, her world had brightened. A new color spectrum from black then gray to ivory to gold had permeated her whole being. She’d lived so long—too long—in the veiled shadows of her marriage, the illness and death of her daughter, then the fear of capture by Vaillancourt. But with her full purpose admitted to Clive and with his encouragement and acceptance of all she was and did, she was more free than she had ever been.

“I will miss your appreciation,” she said with a wink.

“I will not fail to praise you for new skills.”

His risqué words had her laughing, a new phenomenon she enjoyed more and more with him. “Bold man.”

“Your man,” he affirmed in his rough bass voice.

He was hers. No talk of permanence or marriage between them, but still she trusted him. The truth of that was that she had trusted her father, her brother, and Corsini. In response, she gave Clive a broad smile of contentment.

That afternoon, they arrived at the Old Ship. Their trunks and valises, her artwork, were all carried up into the large suite Clive had rented on the top floor to the rear. He had requested it for its proximity to the servants' stairs. If they needed to leave secretly so that she could meet her contact who would spirit her work here in England or to France, then this would be a discreet escape route.

They settled in, content, if not as well fortified by the hotel's dubiously talented chef as they had been by her. They occupied themselves with leisurely doings of living. They walked each morning on the beach. Often they were up and out by nine, running on the rocky shore flying a new kite she'd made, eating ices and little cakes from the vendors who sold their wares in their tiny tents. Just as often, however, the two of them lolled in bed, making love until the sun rose higher in the sky. Each time, Clive spared her the worry of pregnancy. She marveled at his control, for she herself had none. Wanting him once, twice, three times a day, she offered herself up to him—and he came to her, for her, loving her with a tenderness that swelled her heart with pride and joy.

The afternoon they had arrived in Brighton, Giselle had written a cryptic note to Lord Ashley telling him where she'd been, why, and with whom. He returned his own short note two days' hence, telling her he still had no news about the person she would be meeting. Newspapers and those in residence in the hotel restaurant and lobby spoke of nothing but the blockade. Indeed, reports said so many ships sat pointed at each other in that small scrap of ocean that many wondered if the sailors could tell each other fairy tales across the expanse. Both the British and French fleets had so choked up the ocean between the Continent and the British Isles that Giselle thought it silly to even ask Ashley for word of her man. But her duty drove her onward.

It was easy to bide her time and wait for what she hoped would be the end of her trials.

She was at rest and in love.

One week passed, then two.

⇥»»»❬❬❬⇤

CLIVE ROLLED TO his back and checked that Giselle was truly into a deep sleep.

He was growing more irritated by the day. Not in his nature or his habit to be confined to any one place or activity, but this endless wait for Giselle's contact wore on him.

For her, thank goodness, this period was a lull, a reprieve. He saw it in her twinkling smiles and the way she walked into his arms and gave herself so completely to him, day or night.

He welcomed her each time she came to him. He'd never had that spontaneity or that surrender from his wife. Only from a few women whom he'd paid for their service. But that was the picture of his past, long gone now, wasn't it? Lust was a commodity for sale. But intimacy came only from a melding of two minds, two hearts. He would sit at breakfast and marvel at their rapport in or out of bed. This bliss was finally his.

Only if he kept her safe, however, would he be able to enjoy it beyond this day, this challenge, this mystery.

He gathered up his banyan. Swirling it over his shoulders, he pulled it over his arms and tied the sash. She still slept soundly, her mouth open, snoring softly. Chuckling, he would not wake her. He padded into the sitting room.

Just this afternoon, he'd heard from Langley again. Last week, his friend had come down to talk with him in person when first he and Giselle arrived in Brighton. Clive had sent him a cryptic note then, describing briefly—and vaguely—where they'd been. Langley had sent word yesterday that Halsey and he would arrive today to meet with Clive. So the two men must have some news. Clive prayed it was positive. He was so very tired of this muddle of indecision.

He strode to the bureau and poured himself a glass of water, then took it to a chair. In the hall, two people—men—whispered. Not softly enough, he observed with a snort.

They would not be the two men he had hired to watch the hotel and follow Giselle and him when they were out an about. His two men were on duty around the clock outside the Old Ship.

But the two in the hall were much too loud for this hour of the night. What were the staff doing walking the halls before dawn? Wasn't it too early to be setting fires in the guest rooms?

True, there'd been an unseasonal chill in the July night air recently. Nonetheless, he was comfortably warm in his skin and the loose fall of his satin robe. He felt no need for fires to be set.

What were they doing out there? Were they cleaning the carpet?

He doubted they were delivering meals at this hour of the morning. Curiosity spurred him to seek out his pocket watch, which he'd left on the bureau in their bedroom.

No sooner had he picked it up and noted the time of ten past five did he still…and listen.

The hair on his neck rose.

A key slid into the lock of their hallway door.

He took a step forward to hear better.

The handle turned.

Not a screech, but a whir, it was.

He hurried to the fireplace and grabbed a poker.

Whoever they were, whatever they intended, he would not let them succeed.

He padded slowly to the threshold between the bedroom and sitting room, his bare feet soundless as the wheels of eternity. Poker high, stance broad, he listened as they stepped into the suite.

Bad shoes crunched upon the wood. One man hissed at the other.

Clive envisioned them as they walked, one slow foot before the other, toward the bedroom.

He calculated how much room he had to strike one with his iron pike, then how he could strike at an angle to hit the next one. Geometry classes had been useful. Fencing was a better teacher for this.

He tensed.

A wiry fellow darted forward.

Clive hit him squarely in the chest.

The guy woofed. The air socked out of him, he doubled over.

His friend, behind him, jerked to a halt.

Clive was on him, angling a blow to his head.

But a long arm reached out above Clive's head and the hand grabbed the poker, twisted, and yanked.

Clive's knees buckled, but he held his weapon while a third man wrestled with him for possession.

"*Allez, donne-moi ce, imbécile!*" his attacker seethed in French.

Like hell he'd give it over! Clive braced himself and tugged.

But the second man scrambled up and caught Clive's arms while the third man yanked the poker from him.

Each one took him by a shoulder. One punched him in the stomach. The other kicked. Down on his back, Clive tried to roll away. But couldn't.

The other man kneed him in the chest.

Clive gasped for air, but a swift foot to his stomach had him reeling.

A hard fist to his jaw dimmed his sight.

Then next one hit him.

And the night disappeared.

CALLOUSED HANDS SHOOK her.

She grumbled. *Clive?* Clive must have a nightmare.

Giselle reached out for him just as four hands dragged her to the edge of the bed.

Her heart leapt up in her chest. Her eyes opened and she lived her own nightmare. She tried to scream. But a rag was shoved in her mouth and she gagged, kicked, lashed out, yelled, and tried to shove the cloth from her mouth with her tongue.

And failed.

No. No, no, no.

Awake, her pulse pounding, she understood she was undone.

Where is Clive?

Her captors cursed and shot directions to each other.

"Get her hands!"

"I'm trying!"

"Her feet. The rope? Did you… Where is it?"

French. They speak in French!

She shuddered. Vaillancourt's men? She groaned.

She could not go. Would not. They would take her to Paris. She wouldn't live. Wouldn't survive.

Nearly blind with fear, she lashed out, pummeling one fellow, hearing him curse her.

"Naked," oozed one man with salacious glee in his ragged voice as he plucked a nipple.

She recoiled.

"*Ce va*, Maurice. Her tits won't help you bind her."

"Later, then," Maurice crooned as he jammed his face into the hollow of her shoulder and licked her skin.

"Shut up and help me get her out of here. A blanket…or a robe? What?"

Maurice had her on her feet, her skin against his hot, wiry body, his breath rancid and turning her stomach so that beneath the mask, she choked again.

"Mon Dieu, Maurice! Don't smother her!"

"I'll fuck her, though," Maurice said, smooth as ice, his hands squeezing her breasts and trailing down, down, down to…

She squirmed, trying to stomp his toes.

The first man snatched Maurice's hand away from her belly and tussled with Maurice to gain control of her.

"*Merde!*" Maurice shouted as they warred for her. "She's mine. A hellcat. Warm as silk, Franchot. I'll have her on her back for sure before I kill her."

Franchot caught her wrists and gave a mighty yank. She fell against him. He held her in a cold vise of iron. He was dark, smelly, stocky, and strong as a bull. Her gorge rose. She leaned over his beefy arm to spit out the loose rag they'd gagged her with. Then he let her sag, and she sank to the floor like a sack of sand. "Fuck her, Maurice? Ruin her? Kill her? Do that, you fool, and you'll not get the money."

Maurice, quick as the devil, dragged her up from the floor and gave her a violent shake. This time instead of mauling her, he held her from him while his friend Franchot yanked open drawers and threw clothes at her.

"Chemise. Petticoat. Dress." He glared at her, hand out. "Put them on. Quick as can be. Or out you go with us naked. Now you would not want that, would you, Madame Laurant?"

The sound of her name rang through her head like a death knell. They were certainly Vaillancourt's men. Whether the deputy wanted her simply to finish his heinous job of murdering all her family or if he now added to that her false diagrams of English coast towns didn't matter. They had her. She knew not how in hell they expected to get her out of the hotel, into the streets and off to…where? The coast? A ship to cross the Channel cluttered with the hundreds of British and French vessels meant to annihilate each other?

They were either fools or well connected to a network that would take her, pass her from one man or another to another hideaway, another port, another perilous crossing of the turbulent sea to the Seine and Paris, Vaillancourt, and her end in a stone-cold cell.

She caught another breath, hard from the pain in her chest, and let out a sob.

"Do it!" Franchot pointed at the pile of clothes on the bed. "Dress!"

With fevered hands, she pulled on what he'd thrown at her. *Dress, Giselle. Dress*, she said in her head like a prayer, then, struck by an idea, paused when she realized the very dress he'd thrown at her was the most valuable one—the one she'd sewn coins into long, long ago. The gown raised her spirits. Gave her hope and a sense of command. She would survive this. And them. She would!

"Shoes, stockings," she demanded of him.

"Oui. Where?"

"The top drawer," she told him, her shock gone, replaced by a stance that she bet looked like defiance.

Franchot narrowed large blue eyes at her. Assessing her with a curve to his lower lip, he stayed silent as she tugged on her clocked stockings and slipped on the pair of walking shoes he had fished from the bottom of the closet. "Where's your cloak?"

"Folded. Blue." With coins sewn in the pockets and hem, too. "In the chest over there."

He tipped his head in that direction. "Hurry. We get it and leave," he said to her before he turned to Maurice and another conspirator joined them to leer at her. That third man pulled from the back of his breeches a pistol and waved it at her.

She'd not seen that before—and it shocked her as much as their first attempt to put hands on her. She swallowed hard.

"No need for that, Paul." Franchot had a look of disgust on his jowly face. "She's ours. Her man is down, oui?"

"Knocked him out, I did. In there." He nodded toward the sitting room.

Clive! Clive, I will get revenge on these three, too.

"Get her cloak, Paul. That chest there, oui. The blue one. Oui. Put it on, madame."

And keep it close I will. I will! She whirled the heavy cloak around her, then secured it at her throat with the embroidered frog.

"Now tie her hands," Franchot ordered Maurice. "Not behind her, idiot. Oui, now, let's go."

As they strode into the sitting room, her heart crashed to the floor. On his side lay Clive, his handsome face battered and bleeding, his banyan torn and stained, his calves already turning garish colors showing the signs of their brutality. To add insult, they had tied his hands behind him. Even his feet were bound. As she approached him, he struggled to open his eyes. His gaze found hers. They'd stuffed his mouth with a rag and tied it around his head.

His eyes fell down her form, and he blinked, acknowledging that she was dressed. She wondered if he'd heard any of the exchange in the other room.

She licked her lips, wishing she might give him something, anything as encouragement. Yet all she could conjure was a sad, sweet smile that she hoped conveyed how dearly she loved him.

"Madame!" Franchot urged. "Now!"

She pointed toward the large storage chest. "My reticule," she said, pointing to the bag upon a cabinet.

"Non. You will not need it," Franchot said with churlish delight.

"But I do! I have supplies in there. Women's things, you understand, for the time of the month. I need them now!"

Maurice curled his lip and wiped his fingers on his breeches. "*Putain.* I almost touched her!"

She glared at him. At least that man would stay away from her for a few days.

"Bring the bag here, Paul."

The third man loped over and brought it to Franchot.

Dumping the contents on the carpet before them, Franchot bent at the waist. His fingers drifted through the hairbrush, comb, *etui*, white cloths tied together in a big, pale-pink ribbon and a pouch that jingled when he jiggled it. He wrinkled his nose. "Put it all back in there, Paul."

They waited while Paul threw it all back inside and Giselle held her breath.

"Maurice, you first. *Je vous en prie, madame!*" Franchot waved her toward the door. "Bon soir, monsieur le marquis. Happy dreams."

Cur. Giselle gave one last, loving glance at Clive. Then she followed her captor.

Out into the hall and down the staff's narrow wooden stairs they hurried. Maurice. Then she. Paul behind her, carrying a pile of her latest drawings of Brighton—and her reticule, filled with her necessities for her hair, her perfume, and the while strips of cloth she did not yet need but would soon declare she did.

Inside her satin pouch, too, was one other useful item Franchot had not seen. She would hope he never did. Not until she needed it.

Chapter Eighteen

CLIVE WAS GINGERLY climbing out of his tub when a knock came at the sitting room door. He had summoned enough strength to bathe quickly to meet his two friends, Langley and Halsey, downstairs at their prearranged time of ten o'clock. But he was late.

He glanced at his pocket watch upon the far table. Ten fifteen. Well, three men attacking a fellow wearing nothing but the suit he was born in, at five in the morning, definitely meant that at thirty-four years of age, a bloke was a poor wreck of a fighter.

Toweling off, he suppressed groans and grimaced at the pain—and at repeated knocks on his door. He grabbed smalls, fawn breeches, and a shirt, then shuffled barefoot for the door. "Coming! Coming!" he groused.

"Good God," he exclaimed, his shoulders slumping as he stared at Halsey and Langley, "am I glad to see you."

Both men strode in, their brows shooting high as they looked Clive over.

"What in hell happened to you?" Langley winced, closing the door with a quick hand. "The receptionist came into the dining room and told us you had an altercation here last night."

"A polite way to phrase an abduction."

"No! Giselle?" Langley was aghast at Clive's scowl.

Halsey cursed. "Let's sit down, for God's sake." Then he put two fingers to his own nose. "I hope the other man's face is as colorful."

Clive swallowed a wry laugh. "I am doubling up on my visits to Gentleman Jack's very soon." He led them to the settees and chairs, a hand out toward the tray. "If you've not yet had breakfast, please do so."

"You've hardly touched it," Halsey said. "Sit and eat. You look like you need it."

"I'm afraid I've had my guts rearranged recently and I'd embarrass myself if I ate. But I will pour for us all. Coffee, yes?" Clive did as he'd said and passed around cups. He took two sips from his own. "I trust Annabelle and Terese are well?" he asked of Langley.

"Very well. Bella asks for you. We tell her you are traveling for your work but will arrive home soon. Terese is fine, anxious to hear about you and Giselle."

"Have you married?" Clive asked, hoping the two of them had made themselves happy by doing so.

"Terese will not take vows until you are home, safe and sound. I agree with her. Weddings are for family."

Clive tried to smile. "Thank you. You will not share my sorry state with her when you return. I will not have her worry."

Langley grew furious. "Hell, man, *I* worry! I'm surprised you can walk!"

"There is that," Clive said with sarcasm. "I'll go put on a better face, if you'll excuse me."

In his bedroom, he paused to inhale. Calmed by his friends' presence, he was nonetheless irritated with himself that he had to admit to them that he had failed to protect the woman he loved. The one woman in this world whom he needed to save from whoever in damnation had attacked her and carried her away from him—and he had foundered.

He muttered about his need to find her. Buttoning his shirt, winding a simple knot in his plain cravat, he took off hangers a waistcoat and a frockcoat, then ran a comb through his hair.

Christ. Even his scalp hurt. In the warm, soothing waters of his bath, he had seen the damage done to him by the intruders. Not much of him was left untouched. Save his dangly bits. Kind of them, the buggers.

He grimaced, the errant reminder rising, as it had done a hundred times since this morning, that when the men stole into their rooms, Giselle was bare to her skin. He ground his teeth that those hooligans would take advantage of that, abuse her, horrify her, hurt her in the worst way any man could injure a woman.

He cursed beneath his breath and strode back in to his friends.

"Tell us," Langley urged him when Clive had taken a chair and picked up his coffee cup.

"Three men came before dawn," he said with bitterness. "They had a key and stole in. I was awake, not it seems because I heard them, but perhaps because I perceived them or the danger they presented. In any case, when they barged in, I had that poker there in hand."

His two friends eyed the long iron rod on the floor where Clive had left it.

"As you can see, my skills are not up to fighting off so many men at once. I passed out from their attack. When I began to come around, I saw them lead out Giselle."

He would not add details of his state of undress, nor that he'd been restrained with hands and ankles tied. The despair of his inability to save Giselle ate him to the bone. He'd deal with that in days to come as he healed his physical wounds. No need to emphasize to his friends his self-ridicule at his failures. He knew them all too well.

He drank from his cup. "There were three men, all ragtag ruffians. They spoke French. Not Parisian. But Norman. From Le Havre or Calais."

"Why did they carry away Giselle?" Langley asked.

Clive took another long drink of his coffee. It soothed his

weary soul and fortified his aching body. "She has an enemy in Fouché, and his deputy, René Vaillancourt."

Both men froze.

Clive hastened to add, "She also works against the French."

"Not for us!" Halsey blurted, red in the face.

Clive understood his colleague's shock. "No. For Kane, Lord Ashley, and through him—"

"Scarlett Hawthorne," Halsey finished.

Halsey was a tall, dark, severe fellow who was a light of London Society. He had a taste for horses, French wine, and exquisite women. Scarlett Hawthorne—beautiful, educated, and ruthless cit that she was—ran her deceased father's merchant marine business and used his contacts all over the world to run her own espionage network. She did not admit such to anyone, but the successes she had tallied were innumerable. Every day, every night, she was a light of Society despite her mercantile background. Halsey, who advised the prime minister on all agents foreign and domestic, had courted her, as many men had, to little avail. The only man who got close to her was her chief clerk, a giant of a man named Todd Carlton. The other men whom she saw regularly were the ones who worked for her, like Ashley, Ramsey, and dozens more.

Halsey fumed. "How on God's green earth did Madame Laurant get connected with Scarlett?"

"She was childhood friends with Augustine, Lady Ashley, and Amber, Lady Ramsey. They recruited her. For a few years now, she has worked for them."

Halsey's violet eyes shadowed with an urgent fear. "What does she do for them?"

Clive swiftly glanced at Langley. "Those sketches and paintings in the Hastings bookshop?"

Langley nodded. "Yes?"

Halsey knew of them, too. "What of them?"

"Giselle did them. She's executed dozens of paintings and sketches since arriving here in England last autumn. She would visit the town, walk it, measure and define it, then render it in various mediums to place in locations where her contacts picked them up."

"I've marveled at the exquisite nature of those drawings in the Hastings bookshop," Halsey ruminated. "At the inaccuracies in them, too. I thought it was the mistake of the artist. Wondering too why they would be left, other than the fact that whoever was to pick them up saw the mistakes and left them there to rot." He sat forward. "Unusual for a woman to draw landscapes so well…and so deceptively well. How did she learn to do any of that?"

"Ah." That answer Clive had, and it brought a small smile of satisfaction. "When she was a child and her mother was in residence at Versailles, she met her mother's friend."

"Who is…?"

"Madame Élisabeth Vigée-Le Brun."

Halsey stared at Clive.

"That's why," said Langley at last with a shake of his head, "she was invited to Le Brun's party here in Brighton a few weeks ago. They are friends!"

"What's more, Giselle knows the Comte de Vaudreuil and studied with him as well."

"That old roué?" Halsey crowed. The man was responsible for so many scandals at the French royal court that most marveled he yet survived the guillotine.

"He ran fast after the Bastille fell," said Langley.

"Running away with the king's young brother, Artois. Now he's here to grace our shores with his simpering apologias for his sins," Halsey added. "I'd pack him off on a convict ship if I could. He makes trouble for me every time he opens his mouth."

"But he knows a fine artist when he sees one," Clive said. "In Giselle, he spotted her ability to eye a landscape and create a realistic rendering."

"Except," Halsey said, "those Hastings drawings are not accurate."

"No, they weren't." Langley fell back in his chair.

"Because… Dear God," said Halsey, mesmerized, "she is drawing them incorrectly to delude the French! Astonishing. And what is her method?"

"How does she convey them to France?" asked Langley. "She has couriers here in England?"

"One she told me about," Clive said. "Perhaps there are more, but I doubt she knows them all."

"Who is the one?" Halsey pressed him.

Clive gave his first sad laugh of the morning. "A smuggler. Evidently the best. Very successful at running the blockades. He brought Giselle across the Channel last autumn. He runs many a gauntlet through the lines and brings with him news of all types. Useful man. It was one of his whom Giselle was to meet one night in Brighton. But he never appeared. Arrested he was, by revenuers, and so she never heard from any of his men again."

"Who is this smuggler?" Langley asked.

"A fellow by the name of Jacques Durand."

Halsey shook a finger. "I've heard of him. French. An aristo. A prince of the blood. Bourbon, maybe? Hates the little emperor with a blind passion."

Langley frowned. "Does Giselle know that you work for Mulgrave and the Foreign Office?"

"No." Clive had kept that from her. It was prudent. What she did not know, she could not reveal under torture. "The fewer people who know a secret, the safer it is from harm. But to the moment here, we have work to do. Three men to track." He shot up from his chair, groaning as the pain in his ribs doubled him over.

"Hell," Langley cursed. "Are you sure you are able?"

"I've already searched a few clues. After the attack, I went downstairs."

"What? How? You look ragged, old man." Halsey looked skeptical as to Clive's health. "Do sit down."

Clive could not. "I know, I know. But time is fleeting for

Giselle. So I caught my breath this morning, and I hurried to dress. I went downstairs to summon the manager and I demanded he call his staff together. As I suspected, one was missing. A footman whom he'd recently hired had appeared at his regular time last night at eleven. But then this morning at five forty, he was nowhere to be found. The key to my rooms was missing from the front desk, too."

"Does the manager know where this fellow lodges?" Langley asked.

"He does. I had him hire a hack for me straight away, and he and I both went north to the outskirts, to an old inn where the man told him he lived. The owner of the pub told us his lodger had paid his bills and left with his belongings last night. He also had three friends. French, they were. Not a word of English among them."

Halsey frowned. "Did the innkeeper have any idea where they were headed or what they planned next?"

"They spoke of taking a packet out of Hastings," Clive said.

"Bah! Must be a smuggler's boat. But why Hastings?" asked Langley. "Wouldn't you want to bypass the thickest part of the blockade? Why not go to the North Sea, where fewer ships of the line patrol the waters?"

"Hastings," Halsey mused. "We need more than this mention of a trip out of Hastings. But what? What? Wait… Let us consider if this is anything to do with that bookshop business."

"I see no relationship of this to the Hastings drawings remaining in the bookshop. Unless the agent who was to take them has been deterred…" Langley speculated, his eyes widening.

Halsey nodded. "Or knows the drawings or the site have been discovered or compromised."

"And who would know that?" Clive asked himself, and stared at the others. "Only a French agent? Of course! A coordinator. One who has been living here, working here, learning the coastal geography. One who has enough agents in their employ to monitor the bookshop and trace who put them there or who designed them. Dear God. Could that be true? A master French agent in Hastings works among us?"

Halsey grumbled. "It's what I have feared for so long. I've my agents following so many of them, but any in Hastings escape me."

"Who might know?" Clive asked, frustrated, as he paced to the window and back. But he halted. The forces set against his darling Giselle set his mind reeling. "Lord Ashley?"

"Let's go to him. If we must, we'll go over him to Scarlett Hawthorne," Halsey muttered. "We must ask them. Even if they have no idea of a French agent in Hastings, both will want to know what has happened to Giselle."

Langley grimaced. "All the more reason to consult them."

Halsey sniffed. "God knows, I've tried to negotiate with Miss Hawthorne. Stunning, but prickly woman."

"To save her own agent," Clive declared, "she'll want to help us."

⟫⟫⟫⟩⟨⟪⟪⟪

CLIVE AND LANGLEY climbed down from their hired traveling coach that evening at seven twenty.

They'd left Brighton that morning at noon and stopped once to change horses in Crawley. Offering their two different coachmen double their fee to get them to London before dinnertime, they had endured the jostling carriages with a hamper of good food and fine brandy.

As they stepped up to the Ashleys' townhouse at No. 20 Grosvenor Square, they agreed they would not be deterred if the butler were reticent or if Kane and his wife, Gus, were out for the evening. They would remain until they returned and speak of these matters.

The butler was accommodating. After all, Clive knew the man and all the Ashley staff because his own townhouse was at

No. 16. The butler greeted Clive warmly, sensing the urgency of their matter. The Ashleys were at home, he told them. Then he showed the two to the grand salon.

Langley took a chair facing the back garden. Clive paced before the fireplace. He had figured that whoever had taken Giselle was funded well, to hire three men to abduct her. Money enough to hire a fast coach, most likely two. They had means enough to spirit her away quickly and to obscure points of rendezvous with the organizers. The motive could be many things. Clive did not care what it was. He only wanted her back in his care, his embrace.

Halsey ran his own agents in Dover and Ramsgate, but Hastings was the port town he knew most. He'd spent his childhood there under the watchful eyes of his mother and five doting younger sisters. That Halsey knew the area was one boon, but he also knew—courtesy of the women in his family and those who had graced his bed off and on for decades—the society and the military who ran the town.

Scarcely had Clive had time to calculate where the three Frenchmen now held Giselle when the double doors opened and Kane, Lord Ashley, appeared. Surprised and curious, he also had a worried brow.

As well he should.

"Good evening, gentlemen." Ashley strode in as his butler shut the doors behind him. "An honor to have you. However, I note by the hour, you do not call with any good news."

Clive took a step toward Ashley. "We've run up from Brighton. Madame Giselle Laurant was abducted from my presence from the Old Ship Hotel this morning before dawn. Three men accessed the hotel through the servants' staircase and entered my rooms with a key to the lock."

Ashley's face fell as he took in Clive's black eyes and bruises on his throat.

"Fortunately," Clive continued, "Lord Langley and Lord Halsey had scheduled meetings with me previously and arrived in town the day before. Both men called upon me in early morning. Lord Halsey, who parted from Langley and me at ten this morning, has gone to Hastings to investigate as a result of this catastrophe. He knows that town well and thought it best to go ahead of us to find his own agents there. We three probed as best we could early today the facts of the matter in the hotel, and with a local publican who had lodged one of the culprits in his inn."

Ashley paled. "Hideous news. Please do sit, Lord Carlisle. You both appear to need it, and sustenance as well. I will have my man bring in what we have as a cold dinner for you. Now," he said as he went for the bellpull and indicated a chair for Clive, "tell me the rest and we will make haste to get Giselle safely back."

Langley spoke up. "Those of us who work for the prime minister have long suspected that you head a network for Scarlett Hawthorne. We have had clues to that for many years, but of course, none of you has admitted to it."

"As you have not revealed anything to me, sir."

"Quite so," Clive said. "Now, with Giselle gone, that must change. We must learn what you do—not in total, obviously, but at the very least, what you do that hinges on Giselle's work and her disappearance. Whatever you do complements our own work in the Home Office and Foreign Office. We cannot be at cross-purposes here. Now we must learn what you know to help us find her. If she is yours—"

"She is."

Clive rejoiced at the man's admission. "We need not know more from you to help us, but I am very afraid for Giselle's life."

"As am I, Carlisle." Carefully, Ashley had not elaborated on whether he ran agents for the renowned merchant lady in the City.

"I think, sir, we are at first names, don't you?" Clive said.

"Kane, it will be, from now on."

Clive and Edward Langley gave up their own names.

Kane gave a nod. "Please note that Giselle is my wife's dear friend, Clive. We will ask her to tell us what she can, but she will take this news poorly. I ask you to help me break this to her. She is with child once more, and I am devoted to her welfare."

"I understand," Clive said with understanding for a man's desire to protect a woman in any matter, especially one in a delicate condition. A shot of concern zipped through him. His old fear reared its head, that he may not have been so careful of Giselle whenever they made love. Though he had been diligent about withdrawing from her before his own climaxes, he had feared any failure, especially the first night they had enjoyed each other. Since then, he'd been zealous about it. Still he worried. Now more than ever.

"Can you share with me why Lord Halsey has gone to Hastings?" Kane fretted, sitting forward, elbows on his knees. "I mean, does he have another reason besides the fact that he knows the town well?"

Clive quickly ran through the reasons. "Most important is that the three who abducted Giselle mentioned the town often as one from which they would take a packet to France. But Hastings," he murmured, wishing he did not have to speak this next thought, "has another aspect. It is directly across from Boulogne-Sur-Mer."

"You think they're taking her to Bonaparte?" Kane ran a hand over his mouth in horror.

"It makes sense," Clive admitted, his blood boiling with alarm. "Hell if I want to think it."

"In the midst of the blockade?" Kane argued. "Foolish, deadly to try it."

Clive pushed his fear aside and stood, one fist grinding into his other open palm. "Some men care naught for danger, believing in their immortality. But I care not for any of that. I say the only thing now is for us to plot how far and how fast three men with a reluctant lady in tow can travel to Hastings. Then how long can it take to search and hire a boat to the French coast where the Grande Armée resides."

"We must know, Kane," Edward, Lord Langley, spoke up, "if you and Scarlett Hawthorne have agents who work along the coast. A few may be watching those who wish to pay for a quaint sail across to France these days. Do French agents here in Britain have that kind of money? Frankly, I haven't met a rich French émigré in all my life. But do tell us what your information is."

"Most French left their homes with nothing." Kane stared at them both. "But one person can lay his hands on all the gold he wishes. And that man is the one these three take Giselle to meet. The man whose navy she has fooled."

No one uttered the name Bonaparte.

Kane winced. "But there are a few agents in Dover and Hastings. Wily and devious. Two of them are very skilled, and we have not been able to identify them by face or form. Only by description of their actions."

At that point, the butler knocked, entered, and set out his trays.

Kane's jaw set with anxiety.

When his man left them alone, he said, "I know of one French agent who runs five or six others, and we are not able to discover them nor arrest them. However, we know from what we see that all tour the coastal towns and report back to this person."

Clive had to know. "Who is this master agent?"

Once more, the doors opened, and on the threshold stood Kane's wife. A gorgeous creature with huge curls of black hair piled on her head, she wore an at-home dinner gown of dark-rose muslin.

"Good evening, gentlemen," she said with a small smile of welcome as she walked in to take her husband's outstretched hand and sit by his side. "I caught that last. You discuss a master agent, do you?"

"Of the French. Operating on the south coast," Kane filled in for her. "They wish to know what we do."

She bit her lower lip. "It is not much, I am afraid."

"We have tried so desperately," said Kane. "We've laid traps. We get close, we think, but nothing."

Lady Ashley met Edward's and Clive's gazes with sadness in her own verdant green eyes. *"La Mère."*

"The mother?" Clive was stunned. "Who is that? A woman?"

"Yes," admitted Kane with a grunt. "A French mother of spies. We've long known one person has to organize or at least try to collect all information going across the Channel. Scarlett knows it. So do I. Information about her comes, however, not from me. No, this comes from a special source. Mademoiselle Charmaine Massey."

"The Drury Lane actress?" Clive needed to hear anything they might reveal about the notorious woman that many rumored had been a French agent. "She died recently."

"Yes, in great pain and with a guilty conscience," Lady Ashley said. "You see, her youngest sister, Vivienne Massey, who is now Lady Appleby, knows of the name of La Mère. But that is all she knows of this person. Charmaine acted as a French agent here for many years. None of us had any inkling of her actions here in London. When Viv learned of her sister's treachery, she refused to see her ever again. Charmaine tried repeatedly to lure Viv back to her. So she sent her letters, filled with lists of names."

"We have them," said Kane. "We have investigated each as best we can. But, of course, many have fled inland or taken different names…"

Lady Ashley looked rueful. "Or Charmaine made up the names. She was, indeed, a hateful person. We have done the best we can to learn the truth behind those names. We've found a few of those agents. But La Mère? No, we do not know how to identify her."

Clive sought to find strength in this maze. "Langley and I go to meet Halsey in Hastings. I'll not rest until—" He paused, waiting for Kane to break the news of Giselle's abduction to his wife.

The man tipped up her chin. "Sweetheart. Giselle has been

taken from Lord Carlisle early this morning. We believe they go to Hastings. All of us must join together to find her."

Tears dotted the lady's dark lashes. "Oh, Kane. She is so dear to us. A friend for so many years, and what she did for all of us demands we find her."

Kane gathered his wife closer to him. "We will. I promise you, my darling."

Clive hastened to add, "I add my own vow to find Giselle. And after that, Kane, I believe we must share all we know in the Foreign and Home Offices and merge it with all you know through your network."

"I agree." Kane met his gaze with level severity. "Scarlett and I share every confidence. Gus and I have told you all we know. What's more, Scarlett will approve of any method to arrest La Mère."

Clive's relief was boundless. "We leave here tonight. Will you come with us, Kane? Help us root out this La Mère?"

Lady Ashley smiled at her husband with a look of total understanding. "Of course he will."

Kane lifted his wife's hand to his lips and kissed her there. "Of course I will."

Chapter Nineteen

GISELLE'S THREE CAPTORS were quick to action but slow to thought. Wise men they were not.

With her wrists bound behind her most of the day except to eat and relieve herself, she'd spent her last three days trying to lessen the pain in her shoulders. She fought through the agony by breathing deeply and concentrating on any patterns she saw in their behavior.

Paul, a meaty fellow, had the least education and reason. He'd been born in Rouen, a fisherman's son. Maurice, who eyed her like a lascivious bastard, sought to sit beside her and molest her when Franchot was not looking. But their leader was no fool.

He'd slap Maurice's hands from her thigh or her upper arm. "She's meant for better than you, idiot. Keep your dirty hands to yourself. She wants no part of you, I'm sure."

Giselle would take a calming breath at that and return to her focus.

The carriages they hired were those they could afford and as much for comfort as for speed. Afraid to appear too prosperous, she supposed, the men had changed carriages in small towns, away from the bustle of many who might question the wisdom of Frenchmen hiring coaches and dashing away. Making the journey more unbearable were the narrow, ill-kept lanes that led to their destination.

On their third day of travel as they pulled into yet another town, she expected to be hustled out of their carriage, her hands untied, and Paul to drape his arm around her. The appearance that he was her beau or her lover brought wry smiles to her lips. He constantly tried to paw her, just as Maurice did. Only memories of Clive saved her many a sobbing fit.

She'd swallow her sorrows at his loss and force her mind once more to the matter of escaping these three.

From the track of the sun, Giselle could tell they traveled east. None of her captors said why or where. But she had traveled this coast, lived here, walked here, estimated the length and breadth of the seaside walks and beaches. She could tell they passed through Seaford. She liked that small town. So many still spoke a smattering of French, bad as it was, their language derived from the French pirates who, despite the blockade, came in and out of the little seaside town. Recognizing the town pacified her. Knowledge was power. Better yet, she could tell the three could not identify the town immediately.

On the third afternoon of their travels east, Franchot banged on the roof of their carriage and yelled at the coachman to go through the center of town. "Down to the sea."

"He'll never find it," said Paul. "Give him better directions."

"I will find it. Don't you worry," replied Franchot with a glare.

Danger loomed. Giselle smothered the gasp of fear that rose to her throat. She would not let them see her alarm. When they arrived, wherever that was, she would be on alert to her opportunities to use her assets. Her money and the particular item in her reticule, which she asked for each time they stopped to eat or wash, formed the basis of her hope. Now she closed her eyes and waited.

"Come along, madame," Franchot urged her later as the coach idled on a dusty road. He grinned. "Time for a rest. Water. Food. You'll like this cottage."

I doubt it. But her brows shot upward at the sight of a little house of dark stone and brick at the end of a lane overgrown with trees and shrubs. She could not see the whole of the house. It was that large. A surprise, that. Someone long ago had attempted to give the cottage charm. As they approached the house, she admired the clinging vines of red roses climbing one side of a faded ruby door.

Franchot grabbed her arm. "You ready for this next?"

For anything. "Of course."

He snorted and led her the past few steps to the pebbled walk. "Knock, Maurice. Alert our friend."

Someone awaited them?

Not Vaillancourt, certainly. But a conspirator. French. Had to be. Since these three seemed to know no English.

Maurice did as he was told.

"Open the door, idiot!" Franchot jerked Giselle forward.

Behind them, Giselle heard Paul struggling to carry her art. They'd brought along the sketchpads, tablets, and stacks of her drawings, watercolors, and oils on the floor of Clive's and her suite in the Old Ship. That puzzled her.

If they were certain she was the draftsman who had created all the other coastal art, why had they brought them?

Were they to be sent to France along with her? Vaillancourt was no expert in the terrain of the southern English coastline. He could call on experts. Perhaps cartographers in his navy. They would pronounce the art the same or not as those that came before. Besides, had the ruse truly been effective? Well, she concluded it had. Otherwise, why go to all the bother to ferret her out in England and take her back to France? They wished to put her on trial. Or not. Not, most likely. They would take her before Vaillancourt, let him have his moment of seeming triumph over her, then clamp her in chains and take her off…off…

She inhaled, refusing to think beyond.

Franchot crushed her upper arm and dragged her inside the great room to come to a halt before a tall woman.

Well dressed in a fine woven tweed of purple and green, her

hair perfectly coiffed, a few jeweled pins holding in her dark-chestnut curls, she was quite lovely. Clear skin, plush lips, elegance in motion as she rose from her commanding chair and graced them all with a glorious smile beneath an elaborate mask.

"Bonjour, mes amis." She strolled toward Giselle and Franchot, then took a walk around the two. Giselle felt the boring of the lady's unusual eyes, which seemed as though they drilled right through her like two sharp stones of Chinese jade. She stopped in front of Giselle again, her head tossed to one side, and reached out and lifted Giselle's chin. "Have they been kind to you?"

Ah. I am a prize, then. "Oui, mademoiselle."

"Madame!" Franchot corrected her. "Meet the famous La Mère."

Giselle remained passive. A mother of thugs. Did Scarlett Hawthorne know about this female? Did Ashley or Gus? Ramsey or Amber?

If they did, could they find her, and find Giselle? *Oh, God.* What a tangle. Her heart leapt into her throat. Whoever La Mère really was, or whatever she did, the woman would not get the better of her.

The lady dropped her hands to her hips. "No need to enlighten her, Franchot. In fact, the less she learns, the more she will be surprised. We want surprise." She leaned down to put her face much too close to Giselle's. She smelled of cognac and good French perfume. "You know too much of everything. I want you terrified."

Giselle did not bat an eye.

The lady huffed. "Good for you!" she went on in French.

Did she not know English? Or did she stick to her native language for the sake of her three imbeciles? Whatever her reason, Giselle could tell by the quality of the lady's pronunciation that she had command of very fine Parisian French. So then, she was from Paris and had a good education.

"I do like a good foe! You are undaunted, Madame Laurant! Oui, I see you have noticed I do know your full name. I know so very much about you. Even your lover, Monsieur le Marquis de Carlisle. Oui, quite a handsome fellow. Bold. Virile, eh? A good catch for you. Money, power. His connections to the prime minister and with his own agents here in the southern towns. Too bad, my pet, he is of no value to you any more."

As Giselle let La Mère's insults roll off her, she imbibed the importance of what the woman revealed. Clive, sweet man, ran agents, informants for the prime minister. He had not told her that. Part of her rebelled at this. How dare he not tell her!

But then, why would he? He certainly should not have. It wasn't as if she could or would sell him to anyone. But he knew she was harmless.

Ah, yes. He knew all along. Somehow he had seen into her. He had persisted to learn what she did, but through it all, he knew who she was and feared her not. Instead, he loved her.

The realization washed over her like a refreshing shower. Clive was involved in saving England from the tyranny of Bonaparte. *As am I.*

This "mother" would not conquer her. Giselle would leave the lady, perhaps even with a bit of this woman's blood on her hands. She squeezed shut her eyes. *Please, God, let it be so.*

La Mère snapped her fingers high in the air, and from the alcove stepped forward a young woman of twenty or so.

"Suzette!"

Giselle let the name of her little daughter sing through her veins. She might be very foolish, but she nourished the hope it was a sign that this girl would be kind. Giselle could use a friend here.

"Take our guest out and let her relieve herself. Then get her into the bath and wash her." She gazed at Giselle with false pity. "You do stink. Not your fault, of course. But I cannot have that. No lady should suffer such indignities, eh?"

Suzette came forward and waited while Franchot removed the rope from her wrists and tied one end to the girl's.

"Go with them, Franchot. Turn your back on her as she pees.

But if she runs, shoot her."

That shocked Giselle, but she bit her lower lip and held her tongue. *The lady would allow them to kill me? Really?*

The woman sneered at her. "You are a pretty thing. Too bad you are headed for a dungeon. You will lose all that rosy color and rod up your ass. Take her out! Be quick."

Suzette and Giselle were back inside within minutes. Paul and Maurice were busy filling a small copper tub with water Giselle hoped held some heat. She'd take whatever it was, yearning for the eloquent provision of splashing, sloshing water.

"Strip!" La Mère ordered her.

Giselle clutched her gown to her chest. To protect herself, she pretended embarrassment and frowned at the woman. She had faked her monthly courses so that the three men would leave her alone. If they remained to watch her disrobe, they would see she had not donned her apparel for that. Worse, if Suzette took her clothes away, Giselle would lose her coins. "I need nothing from you," she declared to the woman.

"But you enjoy rich attire."

Another fact they knew about her. How had they learned this? She employed no maids, no retainers. Those she had met while here in the South of England were strangers. Only Clive, his sister, and Langley were her new friends—and they were not ones to tell such tales to French conspirators.

"Why treat me well, madame?" She tossed her curls over her shoulders in feigned defiance. "Your new clothes will not persuade me to your cause."

"I supply you with finery to appeal to men."

"I have no desire for that either."

The woman thought that over. "You will if you want to gain favor."

And live? A shiver ran down Giselle's spine. She had watched her sister suffer the outrageous attack of three rapists—and die from their barbaric assault on her pretty body. No one—*no one*— would ever touch her like those men had hurt her sister. She would happily kill them, no matter the cost.

"She'll want to look pretty for Faucon," said Maurice with a lewd light in his watery eyes.

"True," offered the woman. "Faucon may treat you well if you are kind to him."

Giselle sent the woman a look of damaging rebuttal. Whoever this so-called "Falcon" was, whatever power he had, she would give him no quarter.

The woman clapped her hands to hurry her along. "No more delay! Take it all off, lovely Giselle. That gown is ruined. Do not worry. What do you say if we replace this tattered rag with a very nice sarsenet of blue? I will, and soon. You do look best in very pale sky blue. I knew it the best color for you the first time I saw you."

Giselle's lashes flickered. She could not help it.

"I see that you wish to learn where and when it was I first laid eyes on you?"

Giselle would not give her the satisfaction of an answer.

"Ah, yes. Here in Hastings. But you were so involved in your own thoughts, you did not notice me. And that was good. Paul, Maurice, you two go outside. The lady will disrobe!"

As the two men closed the front door, her lady captor swung her hips this way and that as if she danced her way toward Giselle. It was the first movement that told Giselle her female captor was no aristocrat. Perhaps an actress. Or a courtesan.

She put her face in Giselle's again and sneered. "You still have that superior way about you. Your mother taught you that."

This woman knew her mother? How? When?

"I will leech it out of you. Humility is such a useful emotion. Levels us all, no matter to which class our parents we were born. Strip. Get in that tub."

Anger burned into Giselle's veins at the lady's hauteur. But, grateful to have only females for her audience, she did as she was told.

"No corset? Huh," remarked the lady, her full attention on

Giselle's body. "Nice breasts. Full." She reached out and caressed the curve of one.

Giselle set her teeth. *You will die for that.*

"Ever had a woman to your bed?"

Giselle remained stoic.

"Tell me!" La Mère pinched Giselle's nipple.

She lost her breath, but her voice was strong. "Non."

"You might like it. Hmmm. So might I. Ah, but that is for another day. For now, you must wash away the grime of your journey. When we leave here, you will be not only clean but pristine. We like a lady to look and smell like one. Even one who has spent her last few weeks in the bed of her very attentive lover." She leered at Giselle, her cold jade-stone eyes tracing her form.

Her words only made Giselle ache for the sight of that dear man. She prayed as often she could these past few days that Clive had recovered from his injuries. She put a hand to her forehead, a sob of despair rising in her throat. She hoped that no one hired by this woman found him on the floor of their rooms and hurt him even more.

Wherever he was, how ever he was, she prayed he was safe. That he searched for her, she believed with her heart and soul.

Would he find her? Could he?

He'd been thoroughly surprised by their attackers, despite all their precautions and his two hired men. Despite his own connections to agents of his own and the prime minister.

Yet there was hope.

Ah, my darling man, what do you know, what can you learn that you might help me escape from this band of cutthroats?

THE DAYS WORE on. Days grew to weeks. Two, three.

Giselle grew weary of the wait. She was not the only one. The three men grew testy, arguing with each other about who took up the watch. At night, they drank after dinner. La Mère warned them if they fell asleep on watch or missed the approach of a foe, she would see they never worked for her again. She'd send them back to Paris—and Vaillancourt.

Giselle began to welcome the respite from traveling. She was still tied to a chair and to her bed each night. But that was small discomfort after what had come before.

But on an afternoon in the third week, horses' hooves and a dog barking announced a visitor.

"Faucon!" Franchot whispered with glee.

La Mère picked up her pistol and strode to the side of the small window. Using the butt of her gun to move aside the crocheted curtain, she put down her weapon. "Go greet him, Franchot."

"I hope he has a new bottle of cognac," Maurice said with a grin.

"You need none of it, clod," La Mère replied.

"I'll take my money, too, witch."

The four of them had engaged in many an argument over the payment of the fee for their services. La Mère claimed not to carry such large amounts. "Faucon will pay you."

They had grumbled. *When will that be?* they wanted to know.

Now the fellow was here, with whatever rewards he had for his minions…and for his prize captor.

Giselle sat, calm as death, her breathing saving her sanity as she awaited the arrival of the man who was to be her doom.

FAUCON WAS A tall, nimble fellow who spoke excellent, refined Parisian French. He entered the room to fill the cottage with a fragrance of expensive cologne. There he stood examining each of his four cronies, finding fault with each man for some small infraction of bad grooming and praising La Mère for her pretty décolleté and her wisdom to wear the mask. With eyes of green so dark they were nearly black, he was an athletically built man who glided toward Giselle as if indeed he flew before her. Then he took her by her chin and bent close. Too close, his breath minty, he spoke with a relish that was salacious. "A beauty." Then he leaned nearer and inhaled as he ran his nose down her throat to her cleavage. "You smell sweet and succulent. Your doing, is this, Sa—La Mère?"

Giselle blinked. What was La Mère's real name? *Samartine? Sanibel? Sabine? Sandrine?*

"She had to be cleaned, Faucon. None of us could stand her."

"Well, my lovely little artist," Faucon breathed, "I've come to view your work." He whirled away from Giselle toward the others. "Show me what you have of hers."

So this is why they took my drawings and watercolors and oils. To show Faucon.

The three men scurried to grab it all up and array it on every available space. Faucon took his time examining them all.

Finally, he turned to La Mère and grinned. "Well done. This lady is the one we seek."

Did they believe the drawings to be accurate? Or false? Giselle sat, so frozen in fear that she could not breathe.

If Faucon thought them accurate, then the reason to take her to Vaillancourt was for that man to imprison her for personally working against him, despite her so-called good work for the navy. If Faucon thought her work false and the basis of the French navy's analysis of the amphibious invasion boats, the charge against her would be treason.

Either way, she was doomed.

How to learn the answer?

"Surely Monsieur Vaillancourt did not send you to detain me if you question that I am a woman he wants?"

Faucon turned on her with such a vicious look, narrowing his eyes and thinning his lips, that she saw why he was named after a bird of prey. He chucked her under her chin. "Not to worry, *ma petite.* Vaillancourt eats delicacies like you for any reason he chooses."

Well, that was a truth she'd learned long ago. But his answer held no new meanings for her.

"When do we leave this place?" Maurice asked Faucon, irritated.

Faucon sniffed, seemingly indifferent to the man's need for haste. "Ah, well, soon."

So...he has no idea when we can leave. Giselle grabbed a few breaths and, in her heart, warmed to the news.

"*How* soon?" Franchot sneered.

"When I find a Frenchman eager to risk his neck and the guns of the British navy. Want to go in the midst of them? Swim well, do you?"

Faucon left within the next few minutes. He'd come, gone, satisfied himself that Giselle was the captive he wanted, but gave no other news.

Chapter Twenty

"**I** KNOW THIS cottage." Halsey reined in his horse.

"I had a man here last year," said Kane. "We watched this cottage for months. Discovered nothing and no one."

"I've been here, too. Four years ago," Clive added as he gazed at the black-tiled structure with the old, thatched roof. "One of my agents told me about two Frenchmen wandering the beach. It came to nothing. We did not find them."

Today, Halsey had been the one to take the four of them to this cottage on the beach west of Hastings. His two agents, Halsey told them, had spotted new activity here three weeks ago—and so they had continued to spy on the five people who had moved in.

Mallard and Watkins were the names of Halsey's agents, and they knew Hastings like the backs of their hands. Halsey said he had hired the two men three years ago to report any odd happenings in the town. The two, forty if a day, were well known in Hastings. William Mallard owned the largest tavern on the west side. Jim Watkins was one of two blacksmiths in town. His cousin owned the other smithy.

Odds were that all who came to Hastings were known to these two. Even the smugglers who ran ashore could not hide from them. Mallard could tell when his competition took in wine from France or spirits from Holland. The pub keeper offered his smuggled wares with a bravado that set Mallard's teeth on edge. Mallard and Watkins especially appreciated the way Lord Halsey paid them, too.

The door and shutters still held the ruby paint Clive recalled, even though the wood was chipped and battered from the salty wind and rain. "My father brought me here when I was perhaps…twelve? Fourteen? There is a small clearing of trees to the east."

"No windows here on this side," Langley noted. "How many to the other sides, Clive?"

"Only to the front. To the back is a door. A peephole too. A small window sits almost to the roofline so anyone inside cannot see out unless they stand on a chair."

Langley grunted. "Here's hoping they don't think to use it."

Clive snorted. "Or they are all short!"

Kane laughed.

Halsey tipped his head toward the road behind them. "I'll ride back and tell our coachman to wait for a signal from one of us to advance."

"He needs to get off the road," Clive added.

Inside were four rifles and four more pistols. Kane had insisted on extra weapons. The others had agreed they were warranted.

"You worry others will come?" Halsey asked. "I agree. I'll tell him." And off he went back the way the four of them had come.

When he returned, Clive nodded toward the cottage. "Let's take up positions to the east, back, front, and here. Wait until dark and reconvene."

"Hopefully we have a cloudy night." Langley said.

"Ten fifteen?" Clive took out his pistol from his holster and glanced at each of his friends.

In the great room, the three men and La Mère played cards. Drinking, too, since supper, they were boisterous. Having finished washing and drying the dishes, Giselle and Suzette readied for bed.

Giselle noticed that Suzette was tired of tying and untying her to take her outside. Giselle began to ask to go more often. That—along with her promise to the girl not to run—meant Suzette was more willing to remove the rope to both Giselle's hands.

A small victory, but a good one. Giselle still could not access her reticule and the precious weapon she'd concealed there. But her release from her bonds even for a little while inspired hope. She just needed the right moment, the right advantage, to run.

She tired of this endless captivity. Two days had passed since Faucon had come and gone. She was weary of the monotony. Her gown was gone, along with the coins she'd sewn into the hem. Her reticule she'd not had access to. It sat, as it had from their arrival, on a stool by the front door. Untouched by anyone. If she could only get to it, if Suzette would not see her grab it, even with her hands bound, she would find good use for her handy little stiletto.

Suzette called to Franchot to get his assistance to untie Giselle's hands and bind one hand to her own. This was how they went out the back door of the cottage a few times each day to relieve themselves. Franchot always tied a double knot very tightly, leaving marks on Giselle's wrists. Running away, escaping her ties, was not a possibility. Suzette was young and kind to Giselle, but was not inclined to run away with her, nor to cut her free and let her run alone.

But tonight, as Giselle and the girl relieved themselves amid the cover of the forest, Giselle heard the snap of twigs caused by other living creatures. Upon a quick survey of the foliage around her, she noted a set of odd colors, shadowed in the moonlight. She saw not just verdant summer green of shrubs and under-growth. Not just browns and beiges of tree limbs and bushes. Not just blacks of rotting plants. But a flash of a human hand. The wink of an eye. A sharp gray eye that focused on her and blinked twice.

Clive.

She breathed deeply. He had come. He'd found her, and she hoped to God he came with help.

To one side, she heard the scramble of a living thing in the brush.

Was it another man? A friend of Clive's…or…?

She could not wait. Should not. Now was a chance!

She began to cough. "Suzette," she cried with alarm, "I…I am ill. I…" She reached out to support herself against the trunk of a tree. "I had too much to eat at dinner or…or something was bad. Not good." She doubled over. "Awful."

The girl scrunched up her face. "I don't feel sick. Are you sure?"

Giselle put a hand to her head. "Mine was bad." She made herself gag.

"Oh! No!" The girl scurried backward. "Don't do that on me!"

"Cut me loose. I-I can't stand up. What did they feed me? They want to kill me and…and I-I see stars."

The girl yanked on their joined hands. "Come inside."

"No! Untie me! I'm going to lose my dinner."

"Oh! Oh!" Suzette picked at the rope. "Don't do it…don't. Let me! Ugh."

Suzette worked at the tie on her own wrist and picked it loose.

Giselle sank to her knees.

Clive sprang from the trees, Langley with him, and another man, too!

Suzette gaped at Langley, who grinned like a madman and, in one move, wrapped a gag around her mouth. Then he bound her with the rope she had loosened from Giselle's wrist.

Clive had Giselle's hand free.

"Hurry," she pleaded with him, fearing for all their lives.

"There are four inside."

Suzette kicked at Langley, grunting, trying to pummel him. But he had the better of her.

From the corner of her eye, Giselle could see how their other friend crept to the back door.

"Three are men," she told Clive.

"We'll get them," he said as he hugged her. "Stay here."

"No! Have you a gun?"

"This!" He fished in his greatcoat pocket and pressed a small knife into her hand. "If you need." Then he was on his feet, into the fray behind Langley.

"*Q'uest c'est?*" Franchot banged the little door open, and it screeched on its old hinges.

Paul was right behind him. "What gives?"

Not a second passed before Langley had Franchot on his knees…and Clive had Paul.

"Two more inside," Clive told his friends as he clung to a gyrating Paul, but swung at him, knocking him senseless to his back.

Maurice cursed as he stepped into the doorway. It was the wrong move.

Kane swung in front of him, surprised him, and knocked Maurice flat on his back, tying his hands.

Clive rounded the doorway.

A shot rang out.

Giselle's heart leapt into her throat. That came from the front of the cottage.

Clive wove, unsteady on his feet in the doorway. Was he shot?

Langley grunted and sank to one knee. Was he wounded?

Another shot rang out. Giselle turned her head. It came from the front of the cottage.

La Mère! It had to be she at the front door. But whom was she shooting at?

In the melee, Franchot pushed up from the slimy earth and

began to run on all fours, like a monkey in a hurry.

"Get him!" Giselle yelled, but then he turned and headed for her. She threw her knife…and Franchot screamed, holding his bicep, the blood gushing even as he ripped the blade out and, teeth bared, headed for her.

He scrambled toward Giselle, his face warped in pain and hatred. He loomed over her.

Giselle kicked out at him, pushing back in the earth. Gaining no traction, she wrapped her fingers around a nearby sturdy stick.

Franchot growled. With the knife in one hand, he grinned like a madman and stabbed at her arms. Her legs, one, then the other. They stung, burned, and she flailed, aflame. Once. Twice more, he slashed at her legs.

She marveled, as if she floated up and away from her very self, and saw him cutting her, even through her skirts. And her blood, hot and sticky, soaked her skirts.

Pain shot up from her thighs. Blind with it, Giselle lost her breath as the man fell on top of her.

Pinning her down, Franchot squealed with success. "You die," he promised in French as he fought to capture Giselle's hand and sat on top of her thighs to raise her forearm. And there he slashed at her, cursing and aiming for her wrist.

Fury ran through Giselle like booming thunder. With her other hand, she hit at the man. His arm, his throat, his eye.

Of a sudden, Franchot stilled, mouth open, hands combing the air.

Giselle pushed away, out from under him, just as Clive stood above the crazed man who flailed, trying to pull the stick from his eye, yet crying and not daring to pull at it.

Giselle watched Clive. He leaned over the agent and saw his affliction. "I would not, if I were you, yank that out."

The man blinked his one good eye. "This! This!" he screamed, flexing his fingers before his face. And then he fell, face first, into the cold, wet earth.

Clive rolled him over. The fall had driven the wood into his skull. "He's dead."

He went to Giselle and curled her close.

"My legs," she said to him. "And…this…arm."

He tore off his cravat, ripped up her skirts, and wrapped the cloth around one leg, cinching it so tight, she screamed.

"Langley, your stock!" He yelled to his friend. "She's bleeding."

"I don't want to die," she murmured to Clive as she plucked at his greatcoat.

"You won't," he ground out. "You'll live!"

"With you."

"With me," he promised as he snatched Langley's cravat from his hand and bound her arm.

Then the night went black and all pain died.

Chapter Twenty-One

C LIVE GATHERED UP her limp body, a scream silent in his throat. He could not see well in the dark, but he groaned at the profuse way her wrist bled.

Langley rose from the man he'd tied, hand and foot. He stood to one side of Halsey, who stood cleaning his own blade with a lace handkerchief. He leaned against the doorframe, favoring one leg.

"Halsey!" Langley yelled at him. "You're hurt! Do you need—?"

"No! A graze, that's all. Let's truss up these buggers, good and tight. Get our men to haul them to Hastings' gaol and get the hell out of here!"

"I know a house nearby." Halsey hobbled with Clive toward a nearby rock to sit down. "Go ahead. Your lady needs urgent care. Let me bind my wound here."

"Come with us," Clive urged him. "You need tending."

"I am fine. Call upon my cousin in Fish Street. A fine Georgian house, cannot miss it. My cousin will give us one of her bedrooms and call a physician."

"Who is this? Her name, please."

"Lady Tracy."

Langley ran forward to help Clive get Giselle into the carriage. He shut the door on Clive and uttered a few words to the driver, and that man slapped the reins on the horses. "Now we fix you, Halsey!"

Clive could not get to the house and help fast enough. Horror that he might lose Giselle seared his veins like poison. He had tied her limbs, but not stopped the bleeding of her wrist. For that he mopped up the streaming fluid by applying the only thing to hand—a rough coach blanket. In agony, he gathered her cold body close.

"It's not far," he crooned for Giselle.

She heard him not.

But he continued to speak to the woman in his arms, speaking of marriage and children, life in London or Richmond or anywhere else on earth she wished to go. "All of it will be ours, my darling. I promise you."

Less than five minutes later, the hack pulled up to a stone house near the edge of town. A man appeared, curious and officious. The butler, Clive supposed.

"I am a friend of Lord Halsey," he told the silver-haired gentleman as he opened the carriage door. "I need help for my wife." He called her what she was in his heart and for the benefit of any propriety this household upheld. "We need accommodation and a surgeon or physician." He secured Giselle in his grasp.

The man, alarmed, thrust up a hand. "One moment, sir. I will call a footman."

He ran away and returned in a moment. "Do not disturb her, sir, until my man joins us. I've called my lady."

"Lady…?" Clive had trouble recalling the woman's name.

"Lady Tracy, sir. She comes."

As if conjured from the man's words, a woman rushed out. Young, dark hair loose upon her shoulders and eyes wide at the scene before her. "Roberts, call James to help us." She pushed inside, wincing at the looks of the bloody ties on Giselle's wrist and the stains on her skirts. "The wound on her thigh has stopped bleeding. A good sign. But these… Not to worry, sir. We know what to do here."

"A surgeon?"

"Yes. We will send for one. Roberts, we'll carry her into the downstairs library. My chaise longue will serve. Bring it forth. Get Mrs. Howard to bring us bandages, warm water, whisky, and vinegar."

She latched on to Clive's gaze. "The worst is the one to her wrist."

Which still bleeds. He nodded. "Let's get her settled."

LADY TRACY'S SURGEON was a curt, grizzled, white-haired fellow who limped into the room and, without a word, opened his leather kit and bent over Giselle.

He pushed up her skirts, saw the tourniquets and dried blood, then stretched out her afflicted arm upon the mattress. "We must move her to a proper bed."

Clive objected. "No. Help her now."

"Sir, I would like to. She bleeds most here." The surgeon pointed to her forearm, where the bloody cravat showed bright-red blood still seeping out. "This wound is deeper than those on her calves and thighs. I must clean the gash and stitch her up. I need her arm extended and flat. I cannot do that here." He arched a brow and waved a hand at two footmen. "Move her."

Lady Tracy clapped her hands twice, and her tall, sturdy-looking footmen stepped forward. "You will carry her up to the blue bedroom. Mary," she called, and a young maid stepped forward. "Get us some sturdy bedding. Big enough to carry this lady. Hurry."

Meanwhile, the surgeon listened to Giselle's heart, took her pulse from her good wrist, nodded to himself, and tested the blood flow in her legs by pressing on her ankles. Through it all, he hummed. Not a tune, not a high or low note, but one *hmmmm*, as if he were a bee.

The maid was fast, gone and back in minutes with a bed quilt.

Two footmen, under the direction of the butler, slid Giselle into the cover they held like a sling. Cupping her into the cradle of it, they gingerly took her up the stairs to a bedroom on the next floor. There they laid her upon a wide bed.

Clive took her hand as the surgeon—Donald Yarborough by name—bound her forearm above and below the wound with thin strips of leather that he had extracted from his bag. Once he strapped her arm above and below her wound, he removed from his kit a horrendous-looking machine, a tall brass screw with a handle.

"Dear heavens," Clive exclaimed. "What in hell is that?"

"My Petit screw, sir. From His Majesty's army tour of the thirteen colonies. Saved many a life."

"How do you use it?" Clive had never seen such a contraption.

"It screws down on the leather bands. Stops the bleeding, it does. Stand back."

Clive sat with a *thunk* in the nearest chair, silent and helpless, watching the man move with a dexterity that belied his years.

"Lady Tracy sent the maids for a pot of hot water. Bring it here," he instructed James the footman. He mixed salt into a pot of hot water, tested its temperature on his own elbow, nodded to himself, then dribbled the mixture liberally over Giselle's arm.

At once, she bucked. Her eyes flew open and she made a muted cry.

"Hold her down, sir." Yarborough was not deterred by her reaction. "It's the salt. But she comes around, so I can administer a few drops of laudanum. She'll take the cleansing better that way."

Clive winced, but held his tongue. The man knew what he was about.

After the application of a few stitches to her arm, Yarborough pushed up Giselle's skirts, cut them away with long shears, and cleaned her wounds there.

For the next few hours, he repeated the cleansing and the changing of bandages.

Dawn crept into the room as he finished his tasks, asked for yet another bowl of fresh, hot water, and rolled down his shirt sleeves.

"Your assessment, sir?" Clive watched him wash his hands, clean his sewing needle and his iron screw for his tourniquet.

"Her wound to her arm will heal. But it is by far the worst of the four. Those on her legs, as you saw, required only a few stitches. All of them must constantly be bathed in warm water and new bandages applied. All of that will make her scream. A good dose of laudanum will ease her suffering. Do not hesitate to give her another dose. She must not disturb those stitches in her arm, either. Tie her free hand down, if you must. But keep her calm." Yarborough handed Clive a vial of laudanum. "If she becomes feverish, wipe her down with cool cloths. Try to make her drink water and strong tea. No spirits. I will return later today."

Clive caught his arm. "She will recover?"

"She will." Yarborough gave him a quick smile. "Slowly. She has lost much blood. Her attacker tried to slash her wrists. Always a severe wound. But your lady is healthy. Give her time, plenty to drink, broth and soup. Use the laudanum as she needs. Spare it not. Let her recover in peace and quiet."

"The laudanum will not make her permanently addicted?"

"After today and tomorrow, diminish the quantity each time you administer it. I will give you a dropper. Rest easy, sir. Your lady will recover well."

Chapter Twenty-Two

August 24, 1805

GISELLE REDISCOVERED THE colors of her world whenever she opened her eyes to find Clive, tall and dark, a silhouette in grays and earnest hopes, beside her bed. His familiar form remained through many a night, asleep in a large chair into the pale-blue dawn and the gold of midday.

He remained, ever present, ever watchful and smiling, feeding her endless cups of broth and tea.

"You must rest," she rasped one day.

"I will when you are better."

She blinked fat tears away, unable and unwilling to argue with him.

Whether it was the next evening or numerous ones later, she reached for his hand, twined her fingers in his. She had to know how she was saved and if her captors had gotten away. "Tell me what happened."

"We came out when you were so helpful as to feign illness. Three of us—Langley, Kane, and I—heard you from our own posts. My friend, Lord Halsey, was on the front door. We three had little problem subduing the three men, but Halsey was caught off guard by the fracas. When the woman came out the front door, she was firing her own pistol."

"La Mère," she whispered.

"Is that her name?"

Giselle shrugged and gasped, regretting her movement and the sharp pain it sent down her wounded arm.

"Don't worry yourself," Clive said. "Whoever she is, she's a devil. Halsey caught one of her bullets in a thigh, but it is, thank God, more a graze than penetration. What those fiends did to you, I will never forgive. You have been through hell, and I will see you healthy once again."

Breathless, she still had to know one thing. "And the woman? La Mère? Did Kane capture her?"

"No, I am sad to say. She ran. Halsey was unable to follow her, bleeding and limping as he was."

"She was their leader. Save for a man they called the Falcon, or Faucon."

"Is he one of the three men in the cottage?"

"No. He came a few days ago, then left after talking with all of them. He has contacts to take information—and me—across the Channel." She caught her breath, a hand to her chest.

"I wear you out." Clive kissed the knuckles of her good hand. "Rest."

With that assurance, she closed her eyes again. She slept without the dreams of being tied and prodded.

Perhaps it was the next day or the next week when she sat up for the first time, enjoying bread and jam as other questions came to her for Clive.

"Who is La Mère really, I wonder?" she said.

"Do you have any clues?"

"She wore a mask in my presence, so I can say she is lovely, but I might not be able to identify her. Or even draw her."

"You can try later. When you are up to the task."

"I will. I will say that she speaks well, with a Parisian accent. She's had an education. What's more, she claims to have known my mother. I cannot imagine who she might be. But I will think on it, forever if need be. And then…there is one more minor fact. She is elegant in her attire. Why dress like a woman with flair, even though you are a cipher? Does it not make you distinguishable? Noticeable?"

He grew pensive and sat forward, his hands clasped, his brow furrowed. "Her clothing may be one of the marks of her status."

Giselle raised a finger. "One of the ways her men recognize her."

"Do you think she is an aristocrat?"

Giselle thought long and hard on that, only to shake her head. "New or old, I have no idea. But why does she work to secure Bonaparte's success? No. No, don't answer that. I know."

"She may work to remain in his good graces."

"Exactly. To get her lands or wealth or position back—or acquire new holdings."

"Many do," he said, his gray gaze probing hers. "You have worked to defeat him."

She perceived the train of his thought. "My father's influence is gone. The land too. Bought by friends of the empire. My brother is dead. The line of the Viscount of Touraine is gone for my family."

Clive sat forward once more and took her hand. "What you have done for the cause is wonderful. No matter your motive. It has worked."

She saw on his face the pleasure in his words. "You have news?"

"We have word from an agent in Ostend that the Emperor of Austria has joined the United Kingdom and Russia in a coalition."

She jerked forward, her heart pounding in her chest. "Bonaparte will have to fight on two fronts. A nightmare to be pincered between Britain and the Austrians and Russians, too."

"London is pleased that he will have to divide his army and navy."

She caught the note of caution in his voice. "But…what?"

"If he wishes to attack us, we think he will come now. Momentarily."

She squeezed his hand. Remorse had her sagging against her

pillows. "Oh, disaster. My drawings of Brighton will never go to him."

"No, but—"

"I did not complete my mission." She clamped both hands to her lips.

He took down her hands. "Listen to me!"

Tears burned her eyes. "After all this, I did no good."

"Stop this! They have your other drawings."

"Not Brighton."

"No. But that town does not have the best aspects for a beach landing. I doubt the French would consider attacking there. It would certainly not be among the first locations."

She sagged amid her pillows. "I wonder if they have my Hastings drawings."

He expression fell as he stared at her. "What?"

"The French agent who works Hastings has been lax, not picking up my papers. The Ashleys and Ramseys told me that. As of a few weeks ago, before I was abducted, no one had picked up the drawings in a dead drop in a bookstore in Hastings."

His hesitancy gave way to a glorious smile. "Halsey and Langley and I know that, too."

"You know? You…checked?"

"We saw those drawings weeks ago. We left them there as lure for a French agent to pick them up, just as the maps of other cities had been. Since you were abducted, we've been working with Lord Ashley's and Scarlett Hawthorne's agents, so we know all this. Please know your work was a godsend."

"Oh, Clive." All she felt was misery. "We have no proof."

"But we do. Hawthorne's agent in Boulogne confirms that the landing flaps on the amphibious boats are all the same dimensions."

Hawthorne's agent in Boulogne had gotten word to Scarlett of this success?

"If the French come, wherever they come, my darling"—he took both her hands again and grinned—"they will not land."

"But drown."

He stood and bent to put his lips to hers. His kiss was brief and bold. "Rest and recover, my sweetheart. I want to take you home with me to London."

His declaration filled her with a joy she'd rarely felt. "I do prefer your Richmond house," she said with whimsy and a coy tip of her head.

"You knew of me there?" His brows went high.

"Not by name. But by aspect. I saw you a few times in town when I went to buy supplies. I thought to myself then, *What a glorious man. To what lucky woman does he belong?*"

He kissed her again. "I belong to you, Giselle Laurant. I saw you painting, drawing along the river."

"When I lived in the old saddler's house," she reminisced. "After that, I went to Hastings to begin my drawings of there."

Clive would not have her fretting over her work. "My telescope told me how lovely you were, how dedicated to your art. And my heart was captured then as it is now."

She put a finger to his firm lips. "I am honored."

"I love you, Giselle."

The tears she had not yet shed now rolled down her cheeks. "I am honored even more. I love you too, Clive Davenport. You bring to me all the vibrant colors of a life of love."

"Giselle," he crooned, "listen to me. I want you—"

"Clive! Clive!" a man bellowed as he climbed the stairs, his boots clicking on the wood. "Clive!"

A brisk knock at their door was followed by it falling open and banging against the wall.

Langley stood there. His face white. His stance that of a dead man.

Clive shot to his feet.

Dread stopped Giselle's heartbeat.

"What news?" Clive asked.

"Two hundred miles long," Langley managed, breathless. "More!"

"*What?*" Clive grimaced. "The French armada?"

"No! No! The lines of the Grand Army!"

Giselle recoiled in horror. "How? Crossing the Channel? Where? At Dover. From Calais, the shortest route—"

"No!" Langley roared, beaming at them now. "The French go east!"

"*East?*" both Clive and Giselle gasped at the same time.

"Those two hundred thousand men of the Grand Army form lines hundreds of miles long! They march out of Boulogne toward Austria. Boney has declared war on them!"

Clive leaned over and gathered Giselle into his arms. "Success, my love."

"He's left Boulogne," she whispered against his mouth. Then, as best she could amid her bandages and pain, she hugged him. "Bonaparte has gone."

⟫⟫⟫⟪⟪⟪

GISELLE INCHED TO the edge of her bed. She'd been moving slowly for a few days, telling no one because everyone urged her to remain still. Reminding them all she was not porcelain, she recovered her stamina more each day. She itched—no, really, she *twitched* to move.

So here she was, eager for a glimpse of the world beyond her four bedroom walls. Clive was gone to his morning ablutions and had promised to return with her broth and tea.

Once she left this room, this house, she would never drink broth or tea ever again. She'd have roast chicken with potatoes and turnips in gravy. Beef with summer greens. Spinach and oranges, tossed with vinegar and a bit of Italian oil on olives. She'd make bread. Roll it and knead it. Shape it as she wished. Like a ball or a heart.

A heart.

She stood leaning on the windowsill and scanned the

grounds. A small garden surrounded with ruby-red rhododen-drons lay before her. The owner here, Lady Tracy, evidently believed in random planting. The only order was that hedge of red. Lilies of white and variegated yellows sprang up here, there, and beyond. Bluebells spread from one clump of lilies to another. The greens of the foliage ran the spectrum from the pale green of young shoots to the spring greens of new leaves and the glossy forest green of shrubs and, of course, back to the ever-present rhododendrons.

She was blossoming like those red flowers.

She had changed these past weeks, in infinitely tiny degrees, opening to the air, the sky, and a realm of different possibilities. Nearing the end of her mission, meeting Gus and Amber again, reuniting with her mentor and her mother's best friend Madame Le Brun, had begun to conclude her recent life as a spy. They had reawakened in her a desire to create a new life. Her thought of retreating to Cornwall was the marker of that.

But meeting Clive had infused her with a new ambition. Her first thought, that she was not worthy of him—a marquis and she, the youngest daughter of a vicomte—faded quickly.

In its place came a new phenomenon. A reawakening, a birth of a new perception of herself in vibrant shades of possibilities. A foaming white the color of waves crashing on a shore wiped away, little by little, the black marks of her past. Her capture with her sister and brother by Vaillancourt. His man's rape of Lisette and her own outrage. Her marriage, abusive and unbearable.

Those angers faded, washed as if with a soft brush into the verdant greens of a summertime romance. Delicate as a seedling thrusting through good earth, Clive's seeming instant regard for her, his insistent attentions and his charms, had drawn her. Lured her, indeed, with lines of affection, as surely as if he drew them with bold black ink, wrapping around her, holding her near. Watching as if from afar, she had allowed his courting. She had welcomed it. She had invited it, him to her bed, to her heart. That was the celestial blue that had seeped into her consciousness and sustained her through capture. She had not feared death. She had expected Clive's rescue.

And here she was. Lifting her face to the future, planning a new way to live. She needed her watercolors to paint this scene, this time, this moment of success, in her mind.

Three days had passed since Lord Langley had burst into her bedroom with the news that the French army had left the plains of Boulogne. Relief had washed through her with his announcement.

Somehow, she needed more.

Sure what that was, she had used her time awake to ponder what was lacking. Aside from her displeasure with herself at her failure to finish and deliver the Brighton drawings, she wished for a resolution of her personal life. She'd known that Clive had been ready to ask her to marry him just before Langley appeared. He had not broached the subject again, and she put that down to his desire, and her own, to see her health well improved.

She had spent years denigrating marriage. But Clive was everything her husband had never been. Kind, joyous, temperate, a tender parent, he'd commended himself to her from the first minute she'd met him.

For years, not even when she was married, she had not thought of herself as anyone's wife. Certainly not as any man's lover. She'd viewed herself, her life, as one spent alone. Drawing, painting, planting, cooking to please herself only.

She'd even told herself she would live somewhere by the sea, where time and tide blended into an atmosphere without beginning or end.

But that was past. And she was ready now. She loved Clive Davenport. Most wondrously, she did.

She gripped the windowsill and clutched at the handle on the pane of glass. She pushed it open, and the fresh air whirled around her. Fragrances of flowers, grass, and salt infused her with a breath of her new future.

A soft rap at the door was indicative of Clive's gentle knock.

"Come in!" she called to him, whirling around but bracing herself against the sill and wall.

"Good morning." He took one step, saw her, and stopped. "You are up!"

"I am."

His joy was instantly overridden by concern. "Should you be?"

"Yes, I should be. Do come in. Do you have breakfast with you?"

He gestured to one side of the doorway, where he usually placed a tray upon a small stool, before he opened the door. "I bring the usual."

She wrinkled her nose.

He laughed at her humor.

She straightened her back. "I won't drink any of it."

"But—"

"If you insist I drink any of that, dear sir, I will never marry you."

He froze. "Do you intend to?"

"If you will have a Frenchwoman with no dowry, no family, and one skill—aside from cooking, that is."

As if spirited by magic, he was before her, his arms around her, gathering her up off her toes against his solid form. "I will have you, all of you, for the rest of our lives." He dropped a kiss to the tip of her nose. "I have money. It brings me the necessities of life. I have family. But it is not complete. I want to fill it up with you, wonderful you." He pulled away, whimsy in his manner. "In addition, of course, I do like your cooking. I would be pleased to marry a lady who does it so well that, frankly, we will never have to hire a cook."

Laughing, she cuffed him.

He held her so near, her body was his. "In that case, I accept your proposal, my darling, if you agree to one thing."

"Anything you want of me is yours," she whispered.

"Tell me that your mind is clear of your past tragedies."

She stilled, butterflies in her stomach at this that she had not anticipated.

"I am done with revenge. I am done with old horrors. I have used my skills to do what I can for this effort abroad. I will live anew." She cupped his cheeks. "Do you know why?"

He shook his head.

"Because you are my everything, earnest and bright. You are all the colors of my sea and earth and sky. Even the spectrum of heaven. I love you, Clive Davenport. I love you. And if you will have me as your wife, I will rejoice in the thousands of ways you have filled my world with the hues of tenderness and sweet regard."

Tears dotted his blond lashes. "I will have you, my darling. I will have you for the rest of our lives. Never to part. What say you to a wedding next week?"

She slanted two fingers across his handsome lips. "In Richmond."

He curled her close. "You want to live there?"

"When I saw it months ago, a crisp winter sun gilding the white stones, I told myself I could find happiness in its walls. Then I asked in town whose house that was, and to my delight they described the man whom I'd glimpsed and admired his form, his stance, his mien. I caught your title, but then moved it to the back of my mind. I never thought to meet you. Nor have you. Never thought you might care for me, too. So, yes, I would like to be married in your Richmond house and live in it whenever you wish."

"Wherever you wish to be, there I am also, my darling."

TWO DAYS LATER, they stood at the front door of Lady Tracy's home, their luggage loaded in Clive's traveling coach, which he'd had sent from London for their journey to Richmond.

"You have been so gracious to us," Giselle told the young widow.

"We can never thank you enough, my lady." Clive shook hands with Halsey's cousin. "You will come to our wedding, I do hope."

"I would not miss it. Nor would Reggie." Lady Tracy hugged her son close to her side.

Giselle bent to the little boy who had so eagerly come to her room each afternoon this past week and read her his favorite stories. All of them were the English translations of the fabulist La Fontaine's stories for children. Reggie would read in English and Giselle would sit, entranced that this young boy of eight did her such a service.

At one point reading *"Le Loup et la Cigogne,"* or "The Wolf and the Crane," Reggie had wondered what the original book would look like with pictures. Giselle, remembering with fondness her mother reading the same story to her, asked him to get her a paper and pencil. She recreated for him the illustration she recalled in the little, well-thumbed book in her family's chateau library. Reggie had wished to trace her drawing, and Giselle, surprised and pleased by his interest, had helped him.

Afterward, the little boy had pressed his drawing to his chest and said, in imitation of the moral of that story, "I shall always thank those well who do a kind service for me."

She had hugged him to her, telling him she wanted him to come to her wedding to Lord Carlisle, and read stories to a new little friend, Annabelle.

Now he stood beside his mother, his little lips pressed together as a tear slid down his charming cheek.

"I will see you very soon, Reggie."

"We will read more stories, madame?"

"We will, over and over."

"Will you teach me how to draw the other animals in Monsieur la Fontaine's fables?"

"I certainly will. We will encourage Annabelle to join us."

He stood taller with that idea. "We three can write a book and draw the illustrations together!"

"A fine idea, Reggie. I am eager for your visit." And what she told him was to encourage him, but also to see herself as a tutor of those who wished to learn how to draw.

The young boy kissed her on the cheek. "Au revoir, madame."

She ruffled his hair. "Au revoir, monsieur."

⚜

MINUTES LATER IN the carriage, she snuggled closer into Clive's sure embrace and allowed herself to shed the tears she had contained at their departure.

He dug out a handkerchief and dabbed at her cheeks. "Reggie has a good point, you know."

She sniffed and smiled up at him. "I think so, too. It's a refreshing idea. I welcome the prospect. I certainly need to buy all new pencils and chalk. Watercolors and oils and brushes and… I do rattle on."

He lifted her chin and hugged her closer. "Continue, my darling. You should make a list. We'll acquire what you need in Richmond, but if that does not suffice, we'll take a short trip down to London so that you can go to Ackermann's for all your supplies."

She gave him a hearty kiss. "After we are wed."

"Yes, afterward," he said with a wicked gleam in his soft gray eyes.

"We do have so much to do…afterward!"

He grabbed her close and pulled her to his lap, where for the next hour or more, he drove his fiancée—and himself—wild with his affections.

"Doing that in a moving coach," Giselle said as he tried to help her put pins back in her hair, "requires more practice. I do hope we travel often."

He arched a brow. "Ah, but I have plans, and I doubt we shall go far for months and months."

"Staying at home, are we?" she teased.

"Enjoying the serenity," he declared with wicked eyes.

And she kissed him.

WHEN THEY ARRIVED at his modest home along the Thames in Richmond, Giselle stood in the foyer imbibing the atmosphere. The foyer was ethereal. With celestial blue-veined marble on the floor, pink Corinthian columns in a semicircle, and ivory walls that rose to a rotunda of pink glass, she stood in the center of a heaven she had not imagined on Earth.

Clive's butler, an older gentleman named Winston with iron-gray hair and a ready smile, had taken her coat and gloves, then left her and Clive in the hall. The man disappeared, she knew, because he perceived her enchantment with the house's aura.

Clive, brimming with smiles and twinkling eyes, offered his arm. "I am eager to show you the house."

She could not have been more in awe of any building. The foyer opened to a reception room done in shades of pink to fuchsia. To one side, double French doors opened to a grand salon, formal but comfortable in overstuffed Chippendales, handsome settees, and two chaises longue, all done in shades from blue to lavender.

"I am overwhelmed at the colors, the complements, and panache."

Clive might have preened, he was so proud and pleased. "This is my mother's work. She would love your appreciation of it all."

"The rest," she told him. "I must see it all."

He showed her to a long hall, filled with portraits of those he said he would name later, as well as the treasures his family had collected over the centuries from China, India, and Africa.

"The next floor," he said, as he led her up the enclosed marble stairs. "A private place."

Here in a small salon, the palette changed to greens and fawn. Another dining room was small, cozy in yellows and gold.

Then he took her down the hall and stood before a door. "This is the entrance to the marchioness's suite. I had all the previous furniture removed. The hangings taken down. This is yours, to do with as you wish."

"It is empty?"

He was watchful, assessing her reaction. "It is."

"I wish it to remain that way. I want to be with you, each night, each day."

He swept her close and spoke on her lips. "I want you not farther from me than this, always."

Then he kissed her.

She toyed with the end of his cravat. "We could make it our nursery."

"We could."

"Show me your rooms," she urged him.

He led her a few steps down the hall and opened the door to a room done in mahogany and blues.

She strolled about the large bed and waggled her brows at him in approval, then turned for the boudoir, in the center of which stood a large brass tub. His dressing room connected to hers, but she shut the door on that and went to put her arms around his waist. "I feel at home already."

"Good!" His tone was jovial, and she was surprised, as she thought they might take the moment to test the measurements of the giant four-poster bed. "One more room."

Then he pressed a panel in the wall and a door opened.

"A secret room?" She beamed at him as he led her through the door to a room filled with light. "I do like surprises and puzzles and—"

There, placed on the far wall, stood her easel from her hotel room in in Brighton. Beside it stood a comfortable-looking chair, wooden, sturdy. A long table held pots of brushes. A wooden pen holder held pens and pencils. Her bits of graphite that she'd held so dearly stood inside a china dish.

Against the wall, tablets, sketchbooks, and canvases leaned in orderly rows.

She walked among the piles and stacks, noting that she would examine them later. For now, she filled with admiration for the man who stood smiling at her.

"You gathered them all up and brought them here."

"Not at first. I had them brought to me at Lady Tracy's house. I had the staff place them in my bedroom. They were my talisman, to touch, to feel, to absorb the essence of you, to allow me some sanity, some proof that you would recover. And I told myself you *would* recover. You were, you are, my dearest love, and I could not lose you."

She marveled at him, at her good fortune to find him, have him for her own. "You will never lose me. I am yours."

She went to him, and he caught her close, his own emotions shaking his torso.

She pushed away and, with his hands in hers, walked him backward into his bedroom. With a kiss, a sigh, a tender invitation, her clothes drifted to the floor and his followed.

Later, she rubbed her nose on his and told him, "That was much more comfortable than the coach."

Chapter Twenty-Three

GISELLE RAISED HER arms as Terese helped her slide her new gown down over her body. She swayed a bit, still recovering her strength. Still getting used to wearing the elbow-length gloves to cover her scars from the Frenchman's attack.

Terese grinned at her. "A vision in pink and lavender. The silk flows like water."

Giselle inhaled, ready to see it. She'd chosen the colors because those were the ones she wore the first day Clive and she had truly met. It was her wedding day, and she was dressing in a guest bedroom in her finery while Clive dressed in his master suite. It was the last time they would ever be apart.

Happy beyond her expectations, she fingered the silk of her skirt. "You'll do up my laces?"

Giselle had done the same service for Terese yesterday when Clive's sister married Langley in her own salon in Park Street. The newlyweds had waited to leave on their honeymoon to witness Clive and Giselle's marriage today.

Terese got to work on Giselle's ties. But in the glass, Giselle could see her soon-to-be sister-in-law knit her brows.

"There!" Terese cupped Giselle's shoulders and beamed at her. "You are so lovely. Clive is so happy. I've never seen him so happy."

"What bothers you, Terese?"

"I hope you will both be gloriously good to each other."

Giselle's heart paused. "Why would you think we won't be?"

Terese tried to shake away her fears, but failed. "Perhaps I project my own fears on to you."

"What are they?" Giselle took Terese's hands in hers. From Clive, she had heard that Terese's first marriage was a happy one. So Terese's experience was not what bothered her. Giselle had come to know Langley—not well, perhaps. But enough to be able to conclude he was an ethical, kind-hearted man who loved his eight-year-old son, his four brothers, and their families too. More than that, he was besotted with Terese. "Anyone can see Langley adores you. Tell me what worries you."

"My brother is a man of honor and dedication to his country, his estate, his daughter, and you. He will not appreciate that I tell you this. He is a man brought up like so many others of his rank, preferring his personal matters remain private."

"I have understood that."

"I wonder if he has revealed to you the depth of his despair over the failure of his first marriage."

Since she had met Clive, through effort and the joy of loving him, Giselle had left the past behind her. She had the same hope for Clive, too. Old habits died hard. But she knew the path out. "We shape our future from our pasts until we learn we no longer need the old rules."

Terese took that as inspiration, tears dotting her lashes. "It's true. Sometimes happiness comes in great waves. My own first marriage was wonderful and brief. I hope for as much happiness, and this time, I hope for a longer period to enjoy it."

Giselle squeezed her hands. "This union with Langley will be a delight. I have seen you together. I see the potential there. Just as I know joy is possible for Clive and me."

"People hurt each other needlessly. To maintain their pride or—"

"Control."

Terese's gray eyes flashed with a recognition of Giselle's revelation. "I will be delighted and honored to call you my sister-in-law. Shall we go down?"

"I am very ready." Giselle strode to the bedroom door.

But as she passed the stacks of her drawings and sketches, she paused. As if caught by a thread, she glanced down at the collection of her works of Brighton.

"What's the matter, Giselle?"

"I…I need a moment. I…" Then she bent to the collection standing against the wall. Over the past few days, she'd not had time nor the inclination to look at the items standing there. She ran her fingers through the pads and tablets and canvases.

"Giselle?" Terese pressed her. "What is it?"

Giselle shot up straight, her gaze on Terese, but her thoughts, her hopes, flying about her head. Then she picked up her skirts, yanked open her door, and ran down the carpeted hall toward Clive's master bedroom.

There she did not stop, did not knock, but called out to him. "Clive! Clive!" She ran past his sitting room toward his dressing room. "Darling, where are you?"

There he stood, beside his astonished valet. Her soon-to-be husband, handsome in his formal black wedding attire, rushed toward her, his gray eyes burning, seizing her shoulders. "Sweetheart, what's wrong?"

"It's gone!"

"What? What's gone?"

"I just looked at all my drawings and the canvases."

"Giselle, what are you talking about?"

"Oh, Clive!" She reached up, cupped his neck, and stood on her toes to give him a big, smacking kiss. "My sketchpad is gone."

He frowned. "I don't—"

"My smallest sketchpad is not with the others."

He scowled. "I did not see any sketchpad among those I brought from the cottage."

She grinned. "Exactly."

He crushed her against him. "My love, you better tell me what puts such light in your eyes. I am dying here of fright."

She bussed his lips. "Sweet, dear man. The sketchpad is gone. It was small. You know the one. It was so tiny it fit in my palm. I used it often for preliminary drawings. Then put them to scale on a bigger paper or board."

"I still don't understand. If it's gone—"

"But you said you were certain you took them all from the cottage."

"I was. I did. I checked and double-checked the parlor and put all of them in the carriage."

She leaned against him, her arms around his solid body. "My darling man, the sketchpad is gone, and it can be for only one reason."

He pulled back, skeptical yet smiling. "Tell me."

"La Mère must have taken it with her."

Clive stared at her.

She hugged him to her. "When she heard the fighting behind the cottage and saw that her gang was being beaten, she decided to run. If she could not have me, she'd take what she could. That sketchpad could fit in her pockets. If it was not among the other works, it seems to me that her taking it is the only viable explanation."

He stared at her for the longest minute. "You are right."

"Of course I am."

He let out a laugh. "Whatever she sought to do with it—discredit you with Vaillancourt or take it to Boulogne—she has it. This means your mission was a success. In so many ways."

She beamed. "It was." Then she kissed him, and he held her in his arms for ever so long.

"Now it is time for you to marry me, madame. Allow me a moment to satisfy my valet with his careful tying of my cravat."

She backed away, swishing her silken skirts and teasing him like a coquette. "George," she said to the young servant, her gaze still on her fiancé, "don't bother making it too complicated. I'm only going to remove it soon anyway."

Clive burst into a loud chuckle. "Get out of here, madame, or you won't be getting married anytime soon!"

She waggled her fingers at him, then blew a kiss. "Hurry!"

THE GUESTS WHO smiled upon Giselle as she stood on the threshold of the grand salon were a handsome array of friends and acquaintances. They filled the lovely room with such happy faces. The Ashleys, Ramseys, Langleys, Lord Halsey, and Scarlett Hawthorne and her chief clerk, Todd Carlton, were among the number. The blending of the government's and Hawthorne's intelligence agents was allowed by the success of other recent, smaller missions.

They had no confirmation that Giselle's sketches had made it into La Mère's greedy hands. They did not expect any, frankly. If they'd landed in others' hands, they had no knowledge of that either. But yesterday, Clive had had a visit from one of his informants in Hastings. He told of a well-dressed woman of La Mère's description who had hired a smuggler's sloop there, heading for a French port of call. The fate of that woman's counterpart, Faucon, was unknown.

Giselle crossed to Carlisle smiling, accepting that she had done her very best.

Down the aisle, Bella ran toward Giselle. Her little legs pumped so quickly that she tripped in her new shoes. But she rushed into Giselle's arms and threw them around her neck. "You'll be my mama."

"I will indeed, my sweetheart."

Hugging the child close, Giselle looked straight ahead to meet Clive's bright gaze.

"Take my flowers," she whispered to Terese.

Then she took the short walk toward the man she adored, his

daughter in her embrace.

When she faced him, she had trouble controlling the tears that sprang to her eyes. She swallowed, fighting her delight at what they were about to give to each other.

The vicar began the ceremony, and at the point where Clive was to give her his ring, she handed Bella to her aunt.

"With this ring, I thee treasure," Clive said, so low and sultry that she was sure the words were hers alone forevermore.

She repeated the same words as she slid on his fourth finger a gold band she'd had a Richmond jeweler craft for her a few days ago.

"You are mine," Clive said with triumph as he offered his arm and they received the applause and shouted congratulations of their guests.

He walked her through the crowd and led them all to the dining room. There, all the chairs pushed to the wall, the table was laden with every delicacy Clive and she had listed for the cook.

When Clive saw one platter piled high with frilly pastries filled with cream, he stopped to raise a brow at her.

"You made these."

"I did. I want your life filled with all the sweetness I can give."

His gaze widened in silver strikes of lightning. He caught her up, one arm around her waist, and bent her backward with a ravishing kiss.

The crowd crowed and clapped.

"Excellent!" some buzzed.

"Wonderful!" others called.

"Such a kiss!" said someone.

Giselle cupped his cheek. "I love you."

"From the first moment I saw you, I wanted that."

"Because you loved me then," she said in awe.

"And I will until the end of time."

Postlude

After victory at Trafalgar October 21, 1805, the colors of Giselle's and Clive's lives became the rich reds of passion, the deep blues of trust, and the hardy, verdant shades of peaceful green.

When the wars finally ended and Bonaparte was sent far away in 1815, their lives changed more dramatically. Clive no longer was called upon by government officials to serve in espionage roles. Instead, he employed his former agents as analysts to help him run a business of imports and exports.

Giselle had delivered their first son in May, 1806. They named him Henry Armand Davenport, in memory of her father. Three more sons were their blessings every two years, until finally a daughter arrived in 1816.

When Clive's estate manager retired to a cottage on the sea in Cornwall, Clive took over the affairs. In need of some other stimulating project, he wrote a primer on improvements in agricultural production. The book is still sold today as a sound historical record of British achievements in the mid-nineteenth century.

Giselle continued her habit of drawings and paintings of towns and villages, and of the Carlisle homes in London, Richmond, Devonshire—and a new one they had built along the promenade in Brighton. She also taught others, mostly children, her techniques of draftsmanship.

Each summer on the anniversary of their wedding, she and Clive would journey to a new town or village. Their choices were random, inspired by their sense of adventure. They would stay for only a few days, if in Britain. Or if they chose the Continent, they would remain for a few weeks. She would do preliminary calculations and return home, armed with sketches of places they enjoyed. As she finished each one, she and Clive would recall the days they walked the towns and the nights they had enjoyed in each other's arms.

Forty-two years after their marriage and after both Giselle and Clive had returned to their Maker the year before, their daughter Collette—now the Countess of Drewsbury—and their older daughter, Annabelle—now the Duchess of Martindale—threw open the Richmond house as a museum. There, where their father had first seen her mother and fallen in love with her, Collette and Annabelle sponsored a grand salon exposition of their mother's and father's works.

The museum remains open to this day, dedicated to those writers and artists who documented life in the country and in small towns throughout Europe.

Collette's notation at the end of the exhibit was one her mother often repeated: *You come to the thing you love with surprise and a special joy that you have been given a certain gift. You come to the person you love above all others with a reverence. You serve that union with a devotion, each to the other. The blessings of that arrive each day with every smile, each touch of the hand, each tear shed together through loss and hardship, and each triumph brings new astonishment, new gratitude and peace.*

Travels with Cerise

The D-Day invasion of Normandy was a valiant amphibious endeavor by a combined force of allies to defeat an enemy.

But that event—composed of convoys of ships, submarines, air defense, and airmen, soldiers, and marines—was not the first such invasion of one country.

Napoleon ordered an invasion of England's southern coast in the summer of 1805. Preparing for air, land, and sea assault, he had all kinds of weaponry made. Hot air balloons, tunnel-digging machinery, and a flotilla of amphibious landing gear similar to what you see in film of D-Day soldiers on flat-bottomed boats evacuating into the open waves.

The French emperor had wanted such an invasion for many years. He encouraged his admirals to strike British shipping, naval and commercial. But he was met with defeat many times. Bemoaning his admirals' "whining and delays," he pushed them into conflicts they could not win. For a show of strength, he assembled two hundred thousand soldiers of his Grand Army in Boulogne along the Normandy coast and held maneuvers with soldiers shouting and chanting, taunting their enemy across the waves. The noise carried across the Channel and sent thousands of English residents fleeing with their possessions. Only a few braved the seashore for brief holidays.

Against this reality, LORD CARLISLE'S ENTICING LURE in my SCARLETT AFFAIRS series highlights this threatened invasion—amidst a romance that I hope has thrilled you with its charm and torment.

Here you read of Madame Élisabeth Vigée-Le Brun, the portraitist to so many royals, including Marie Antoinette. In truth, the lady did visit Brighton in the summer of 1805. She did hear the Grand Army shouting across the Channel and she was frightened of it. She did also hate that the English weather clogged her oils, and so while there, she worked in watercolors.

Is it possible that someone like Giselle could make drawings that might influence the design of French boats? Especially the amphibious landing boats Napoleon wanted for the English coastal invasion?

It is possible. Why is that? French naval designers were not trained, qualified shipwrights. They were not as practiced on the sea as they should have been. Their "scientific principles" were not only wrong, says one scholar, but deadly to the crew. They tended to focus on the design of the hull to make the ship run faster. But their calculations were such that the internal framing was not adequate to support the bulk of the ship. Many vessels took on water, threatening to capsize.

While we have no evidence someone like Giselle designed drawings of coastal towns to dupe the French into the poor design of their amphibious boats, it is true that the landing craft they did design had flaps that, once down, would have drowned the soldiers on board.

The French did not try to invade that summer, but in August the Grand Army turned toward Central Europe to fight a new coalition of enemies. Months later, October 21, 1805, Admiral Nelson met the French at Trafalgar, and for more than a century thereafter claimed the oceans for the British.

Thank you for reading my series! We are on to 1806 and a bemused Lord Halsey, who is enchanted with a lady who refuses him as no other lady ever has. Will he allow her to elude him—or learn that she really does find him alluring for reasons he cannot imagine?

Happy Reading!
Cerise

About the Author

Cerise DeLand loves to write about dashing heroes and the sassy women they adore. Whether she's penning historical romances or contemporaries, she has received praise for her poetic elegance and accuracy of detail.

An award-winning author of more than 50 novels, she's been published since 1991 by Pocket Books, St. Martin's Press, Kensington and independent presses. Her books have been monthly selections of the Doubleday Book Club and the Mystery Guild. Plus she's won nominations and awards for Best Historical of the Year, Best Regency and scores of rave reviews from *Romantic Times, Affair de Coeur, Publisher's Weekly* and more.

To research, she's dived into the oldest texts and dustiest library shelves. She's also traveled abroad, trusty notebook and pen in hand, to visit the chateaux and country homes she loves to people with her own imaginary characters.

And at home every day? She loves to cook, hates to dust, goes swimming at least once a week and tries (desperately) to grow vegetables in her arid backyard in south Texas!